Katy Birchall is the author of the side-splittingly funny
The It Girl: Superstar Geek, *The It Girl: Team Awkward*,
The It Girl: Don't Tell the Bridesmaid and the Hotel Royale
series, *Secrets of a Teenage Heiress* and *Dramas of a Teenage
Heiress*. She collaborated with Alesha Dixon on the bestselling
Lightning Girl and *Star Switch* series, and with YouTube stars
Lucy and Lydia Connell on their teen series, *Find the Girl*.
Katy was proud to be the author of a retelling of Jane Austen's
Emma for the *Awesomely Austen* series, a collection of Austen's
novels retold for younger readers. She also works as a freelance
journalist and has written a non-fiction book, *How to be a
Princess: Real-Life Fairy Tales for Modern Heroines*.

Katy won the 24/7 Theatre Festival Award for Most Promising
New Comedy Writer with her very serious play about a ninja
monkey at a dinner party.

When she isn't busy writing, she is reading biopics
of Jane Austen, daydreaming about being an elf in *The Lord of
the Rings*, or running across a park chasing

Published in the UK by Scholastic Children's Books, 2020
Euston House, 24 Eversholt Street, London, NW1 1DB
A division of Scholastic Limited

London – New York – Toronto – Sydney – Auckland
Mexico City – New Delhi – Hong Kong

Text © Katy Birchall, 2020
Cover art by Jane Pica © Scholastic, 2020

ISBN 978 1407 19650 3

A CIP catalogue record for this book
is available from the British Library.

Printed by CPI Group (UK) Ltd, Croydon, CR0 4YY
Papers used by Scholastic Children's Books are made
from wood grown in sustainable forests.

This is
and dialo
fictitio

KATY BIRCHALL

Morgan Charmley

Spells and Secrets

★

For Sam, Luke, Thomas,
Lily and Ted

★

CHAPTER

✦ One ✦

"Do you believe in witches?"

I jump at the question, spilling my drink all over me.

"WHAT? *Witches?* NO!" I squeak, staring wide-eyed at Kareen, who has asked the question. "Don't be RIDICULOUS! That is so stupid! Seriously, *witches?*" I gesticulate wildly, the homemade lemonade dribbling down my fingers. "That's crazy talk, Kareen! That's MAD!" I tip my head back and cackle loudly for effect, before adding, "There's no such thing as witches. Everyone knows that. So, *no*, I do not believe in witches."

Silence descends. Kareen makes a face at me.

"Thanks for your opinion, Morgan," she says with a sneer, "but I wasn't asking you."

"Oh."

Zoey and Lucy, in on the conversation, snigger together. Heat rises to my cheeks as I realize my embarrassing mistake. I'm an idiot. She wasn't even looking at me when she asked the question. Now that I think about it, I'm not even sure she'd noticed I was there.

"Sorry," I say quietly, my eyes falling to the floor.

"Why are you asking about witches?" Zoey asks, flicking her hair behind her shoulders and going back to ignoring me.

"Iris keeps talking about them," Kareen says breezily, as I sip what's left of my drink. "I think she's met one."

I spit my lemonade out everywhere, coughing and spluttering.

"EW!" Lucy cries, recoiling from the spray. "Gross!"

"Sorry," I say again, my eyes watering from the liquid going up my nose. "What was that you said about Iris? She's met a witch? That's impossible."

"Well, *I* think she has," Kareen explains to me reluctantly, clearly wishing I'd leave them alone. "She keeps having the same dream about seeing a witch perform magical spells, you know, a recurring dream. Anyway, it's so detailed and real that I said to her maybe she had met a witch – " her eyes widen with excitement – "and then they'd wiped her memory but not done it properly. So now, she keeps dreaming about something she's actually seen. That happens in TV shows and movies all the time."

"No way." Zoey laughs, rolling her eyes. "Don't be stupid, Kareen."

"Yeah, Kareen," I agree, nodding vigorously, "don't be stupid."

Kareen narrows her eyes at me and I take that as my cue to leave. I make an excuse about getting another drink and then slip through the crowded kitchen, heading down the hall where party guests are chatting and laughing together, before ducking into an empty room and shutting the door behind me. My heart is thudding loudly as I lean back against the door, feeling sick to my stomach.

Kareen isn't stupid. She isn't stupid at all. In fact, she's right.

I know that Iris has met a witch. I know that Iris saw the witch performing magical spells. I know that the witch then wiped Iris's memory using an amateur warlock's potion.

I *know* all this.

Because that witch happens to be me.

I shouldn't have come to this party. This is all Mum's fault. She's the one who encouraged me to go. When

3

Iris, the most popular girl in my class, messaged me just before Christmas and invited me to her New Year's Eve party, I thought she had accidentally messaged the wrong person, and so I replied to let her know her mistake. She'd then messaged some laugh emojis before telling me that there wasn't a mistake, she really did want me to come if I didn't already have plans.

"That's wonderful!" Mum had exclaimed when I told her I'd been invited to a party. "You see? I told you that the events of last term would soon be forgotten. No one could stay mad at you. All is well and you'll start the new term afresh."

"Mum, you are deluded," I'd said stubbornly. "I am not going to this party. And I'm grounded, remember? You grounded me for the Christmas holidays."

"Well, I'm setting you free," she'd said cheerily. "Why wouldn't you want to go? Things aren't that bad, are they?"

Yes, Mum, things are that bad. Things are *very* bad. In fact, things could not be WORSE.

When I passed my Young Witch Exam, or YWE, in the summer, proving I was in control of my magical powers and could therefore go to normal school without the risk of revealing the secret that witches exist, I was *ecstatic*. I'd been home-schooled FOR EVER, tutored by

Mum's friend and fellow witch Dora, and I was desperate to go to school and have the chance to make friends. Most witches pass their YWE at the age of five. I was a bit behind so by the age of thirteen, I'd yet to make one friend. Not one. Every year, my birthday parties consisted of my mum, Dora and her husband, Howard. And Howard doesn't know that he's married to a witch, so most of the time we couldn't even do anything cool and magical. We'd all sit around in our party hats, eating cake and playing charades. One disastrous year, Mum tried to mix it up and we all went roller-skating.

I rolled into a bin and knocked out a tooth.

I don't want to talk about it.

Anyway, the point is, I couldn't WAIT to go to school and be around people my own age. From the very first day, I promised Mum that I wouldn't use any spells because obviously it would be really bad if any normal students found out that witches live among them blah blah blah. And I fully intended to stick to that promise. Trust me, you do not want to cross my mum. She is, ever so slightly, terrifying. Not only is she this fiercely intelligent, super-authoritative businesswoman, CEO of an advertising company, she is also the Great Sorceress of the witch community, the youngest EVER to be voted into that position. So I wasn't planning on letting her down. I was determined to be on my best behaviour, stick to the rules and glide through my school years, making hordes of friends and passing myself off as a perfectly normal student.

Unfortunately, things didn't quite work out that smoothly. I wasn't exactly well-practised in the whole making-friends arena and within a few weeks of the start of my very first term, I realized I would have to cast a few harmless, teeny-tiny spells if I was ever going to have a shot at fitting in.

But some of the magic got a little bit out of control, like how I forced the headmaster to uncontrollably salsa dance all the time, everywhere he went. Or how a swarm of bats I summoned to scare my classmate, Felix, ended up trapping him and his family inside their house for a few weeks – an issue that I made worse when I tried to get rid of the bats and instead turned them into mini dragons.

Yeah. It was bad.

The worst thing, though, wasn't the dragon situation. The worst thing was that I used my magic to become amazing at dancing to impress my talent-show team. Zoey, Kareen, Lucy and Iris all thought I was some kind of professional breakdancer and we became best friends as I fooled them into thinking that we were going to win the show. Then, at the last minute, I backed out and they had to go on stage and perform to a huge audience with a team member down and without any rehearsal. Unsurprisingly, they now hate me.

I could have gone through with the talent show, too, and then I'd still be wildly popular. Even though my magic was starting to wane – no magic lasts for ever – I had a secret weapon: dance potion from a warlock. But that stupid warlock basically guilted me into doing "the right thing", arguing that I was lying to myself and to everyone else by using magic to cheat.

Ugh, warlocks are the worst.

How come I manage to find the one warlock in the WORLD who is a nice person? And not just that, but he encourages *me* to be a nice person, too. It makes everything so much more confusing, and my life is already a DISASTER.

Witches and warlocks are enemies. We have been for centuries. It's the way the world is. Witches can create powerful magic by clicking their fingers (which is awesome). Warlocks, on the other hand, make stupid magical potions in their smelly, gross cauldrons (which is obviously lame).

Witches HATE warlocks. Warlocks HATE witches. And that's that. No questions. Simple.

Of course, I have to go and mess everything up by being friends with one.

I blame Owen Blaze, the warlock in question. It's not my fault that he happens to go to my school and be in the same class. And it's also not my fault that we each discovered what the other secretly was. If we're going to point fingers at anyone, I vote pointing the finger at him. He could have stayed out of my business and let me go on causing chaos at school by using magic, but *nooooo*, he HAD to get involved and be all nice about it and help me.

Now, it's very hard not to like him.

"Go to the party, Morgan, it will be fine," Mum had said with a long, drawn-out sigh, once I'd listed all the above reasons to outline why I shouldn't show my face at a school party. EXCEPT the part about Owen.

Mum can never find out that I am friends with Owen Blaze. Ever. She would *kill* me.

It's bad enough that I have to put up with the constant snide comments about our friendship from my familiar, Merlin. Every witch has a familiar, a shape-shifting animal spirit guide, who is always with you, supposedly your soul's sidekick, advising and supporting you through life.

Yeah, it's a lovely idea, except while every other witch on the planet seems to have a kind-hearted familiar, I've been landed with grumpy Merlin, who is sarcastic and rude at the best of times.

"Everyone will stare meanly at me and whisper about me behind my back. They hate me," I'd cried at Mum, while Merlin took the form of a bat and sat happily on top of my head, digging his gross bat talons into my scalp. "OUCH, MERLIN! Get off."

I'd swung my arm up at him but he'd flitted away, leaving me to hit myself in the head.

He'd screeched with laughter, receiving a glare from Mum's familiar, Helena, who had been in the form of an elegant Bengal cat, sitting by Mum's feet. Merlin had ignored Helena's looks and flown back to perch on my head again.

"Morgan Charmley," Mum had said, coming over to put her hands on my shoulders, "your schoolmates do not hate you."

"They think I'm a horrible person for letting down Iris and the other girls right before the talent show."

"Go prove them wrong. Show them you're not a horrible person and have fun at the party. You have to face them some time. They became your friends last term. It won't be long until you're all friends again."

"They were friends with me because I used magic to fool them into thinking I was cool."

"They were friends with you because of *who you are*," Mum had said, looking me straight in the eye and beaming at me. "It had nothing to do with magic."

Obviously, Mum was wrong, but we were having a nice mother-daughter moment and I didn't want to spoil it by pointing that out.

Now, here I am at this party trying to prove that I'm not a horrible person. So far, I've managed to spit my drink all over the girls I'm supposed to be making it up to and now I've shut myself away in an empty room, so it hasn't really gone that well.

Merlin, who has been in the form of an ant hiding underneath my collar, changes into a tarantula and crawls down my arm under my sleeve, appearing on my hand.

He rolls all eight of his eyes at me.

"I know, I know," I sigh. "You don't need to say it. This is a lost cause and I should go home before I embarrass myself any further."

"Morgan?" a voice says suddenly from the other side of the room.

I yelp in surprise; Merlin disappears, turning into a fly and zipping back under my sleeve before he can be seen.

A head pops up from the sofa.

"Iris!" I cry out, placing a hand on my chest. "What are you doing in here?"

She sits up properly on the sofa. "Hey, Morgan."

"You gave me a heart attack! I thought I was alone!"

"It's weird," she says, crossing her arms and raising her eyebrows at me, "but I could have *sworn* you were just talking to a spider."

CHAPTER

✦ Two ✦

Iris stares suspiciously as she gets up from the sofa and comes towards me.

"Talking to a spider? Don't be silly!" I laugh. "Must have been a trick of the light!"

"But you were talking to someone and I thought I saw..."

She trails off, her forehead creased in confusion. Even though we're in the same class, I'm always amazed at how much more grown-up Iris looks compared to me. She's wearing a silver sequin top with black skinny jeans and heeled boots. She's pinned back one side of her long, curly dark hair, so that it's swept behind her neck, cascading down the other shoulder, and she's wearing barely-there eye make-up with bright red lipstick, completing her perfect, sophisticated look.

I am wearing an oversized jumper, jeans and scuffed trainers. Right before I left to come to the party, Merlin was sitting on my desk in the form of a skunk and he took a look at me and went, "So, we're not going to the party, then?"

"Yes, we are. We're going now."

"Oh. OK. As in, you're going like that?"

"Yes."

"Dressed in those clothes?"

"Yes."

"Wearing what you're wearing now?"

"Yes."

"That outfit?"

"What's wrong with it?"

"Nothing."

"Good."

"If you don't mind looking like you've given up on hygiene."

"I look *fine*."

"Sure."

"It's casual chic."

"You need some perfume?" He'd turned round and lifted his tail. "I think it will match the look you're going for."

13

This is the sort of thing I have to put up with on a daily basis. Most witches would be encouraged by their familiars to express themselves however they wish to. The other day I overheard Helena telling Mum that she was the most beautiful witch in the world.

Merlin once told me I have the look of an alien.

"It's the shape of your head," he'd pondered aloud. "And something about you facially."

Although there's nothing I can do about the shape of my head, I do wish I'd maybe put a bit more effort into my outfit now that I'm standing here in front of a very glamorous Iris. But I'd wanted Mum to know that I wasn't happy AT ALL about going to this party and I was only going because she was forcing me to leave the house.

"I guess it doesn't make any sense that you'd be talking to a spider," Iris says eventually, still deep in thought, her eyebrows knitted together.

"Maybe your brain was playing tricks on you because of what happened on my first day last term," I point out with a nervous laugh. "Remember that? When I accidentally brought my pet spider to school?"

I wince just speaking about that incident out loud. Merlin had got overexcited and crawled out in front of everyone in the school hallway, in his tarantula form. I still blame that crucial moment for everything that happened afterwards. Maybe if people hadn't thought I was a total freak who brought a tarantula into school, they would have been more inclined to be my friend.

"I promise I don't have my spider on me." I laugh, holding up my hands. "I would never bring him to your party. He is safely at home in his cage."

I hear a small voice hiss from my sleeve, "Or is he? Mwahaha!"

If he dares...

"Sorry, you're right. I must have been seeing things," Iris says, shaking her head.

"It didn't help that I was talking to myself out loud. I do that quite a lot."

"Me too," she says, still frowning.

"I'm sorry I disturbed you," I say, gesturing to the sofa. "Are you OK?"

"Yeah, I'm fine. I came in here to get away from the noise and busyness for a bit. I've been having these weird dreams lately and not sleeping well and—" She hesitates, before collecting herself and smiling at me. "Sorry, I don't mean to ramble. It's weird that I came in here to hide from my own party."

"It doesn't seem weird to me," I say with a shrug. "I also came in here to hide. I spat my drink out over Kareen, Lucy and Zoey."

"Ah." She tries to stifle a laugh. "I bet they loved that."

"And I thought it wasn't possible for them to hate me any more than they already did."

We share a smile. Despite the rest of the school being mad at me for letting down Iris, she is, surprisingly, not mad about it at all. She thinks that I did her a favour because it meant that she was able to be centre stage and go on to win the competition. I don't want to get ahead of myself but I *think* we're sort-of friends now.

Although, she may not want to be if she ever finds out that I was the one who wiped her memory.

"So, what was that you were saying about weird dreams?" I ask breezily, desperate for more information. It would be good to know how much trouble I might be in.

"Don't worry about it," she says, brushing my question aside with a wave of her hand. "It's boring. We should get back to the party."

"Thanks so much for inviting me. It's lots of fun."

"Good," she says, reaching round me to open the door. "There are going to be fireworks soon. Don't miss them."

She leaves the room and there's an eruption of cheers and whoops from a large group standing in the hallway, eagerly bringing her into their loud conversation as music blares through the speakers. I come back into the hall completely unnoticed and ignored, finding myself wandering through the house, not sure where I'm planning on going.

"Morgan! Over here!"

I grin broadly at the sound of Owen's voice, spotting him in the corner of the kitchen with Felix. I make my way towards them, pleased to have an ally at last.

"Happy new year!" I say, joining them. "How's it going?"

"Felix is in a bad mood because he's already got detention even though the new term hasn't started," Owen tells me, while Felix stands next to him looking bored of my company already.

"How is that even possible?" I ask, mildly impressed.

"He was caught trying to break into the headmaster's office during the school dance at the end of last term."

"Wow."

"Maybe I wouldn't have been caught if my *friend* had been there as lookout, rather than wasting time talking to you," Felix says pointedly, giving me a disgusted look. "I'm going to go get ready for the fireworks. Maybe Iris's dad will let me light one."

"Yeah, good luck with that," Owen calls after him as he walks away, before turning to me with an apologetic smile. "He can be a real idiot sometimes."

"You mean there are times when he's not an idiot?" I raise my eyebrows. "I find that hard to believe."

Owen grins at me. "Where's Merlin? Is he going to make a sudden appearance this evening and freak out everyone in the room?"

"He's under strict instructions not to ruin my life again. He is currently . . . uh—" I realize that I can't feel him on my arm any more and start to panic. "Where is that little. . ."

"OUCH!" Owen's hand flies to his neck.

I spot Merlin as a wasp hovering behind Owen's head, sniggering.

"Merlin," I hiss angrily. "Get back here. Now."

Merlin reluctantly buzzes back to me, landing on my shoulder, taking the form of a spider again.

"Sorry," I say to Owen as he glares at Merlin's hairy legs disappearing under my collar. "You know he's not a fan of—"

"Warlocks, I know," he grumbles. "Trust me, the feeling is mutual."

"At least he didn't turn into a lion and bite your arm off," I say brightly. "He mentioned to me the other day that he might do that when he next saw you."

"How generous of him to resist the temptation."

"I'm really sorry. It's not cool. I'll have a word with him."

"If you could." He sighs, before his mouth twitches into a smile again. "So, how was your Christmas?"

"Great," I say excitedly, glancing round to make sure no one can hear. "Mum made it snow inside and turned the stairs into a ski slope, so we learned how to snowboard. Then we toasted marshmallows on a bonfire she created in the sitting room."

"Right." Owen takes a sip of his Coke. "Just your average Christmas, then."

"It must suck not being a witch," I say, giving him a sympathetic look. "What do warlocks do for Christmas? Attempt to make a potion that somehow makes warlocks cool for the day?"

He rolls his eyes as I give him a smug smile.

"Actually, we had a very traditional, normal Christmas. My dad doesn't know he's married to a warlock, remember?"

"Oh yeah." I nod, feeling quite lucky that I don't have a normal parent to spoil all the fun I can have with Mum. "That's rubbish."

"Not really. On Boxing Day, we pretended that we were going to do some shopping while he looked after the bookshop. Instead, Mum and I took some potion she'd made specially, and we became the best pilots in the world for a day. We borrowed some jets. Best day of my life. It was like being in *Top Gun*." He reaches over and puts a hand on my shoulder. "I guess a warlock Christmas sounds better than a witch one."

I shake his hand off grumpily, annoyed that I didn't think to ask Mum if we could fly jet planes around really fast. "Whatever. Warlocks are ... stupid."

He smiles mischievously. "Good one."

"Actually, I mean it." I check that Iris isn't nearby. "You know that potion you made to wipe Iris's memory when she saw us performing those magic spells at the school dance? It didn't work."

His eyes widen in fear. "Seriously? She knows?"

"Sort of. She's having dreams about it, but she doesn't know that it was real. Your rubbish potion only blurred her memory. It was supposed to make her forget altogether."

"Firstly, you were the one doing the magic at school, not me," he hisses defensively. "And secondly, memory-wiping potion is difficult to get right, and I'm still learning, remember?"

"Yeah, well maybe you should have checked it was correct before you slipped it in her smoothie," I huff.

"Maybe you shouldn't have sent a swarm of bats after Felix and then turned them into mini dragons chilling in a tree in the middle of Essex."

UGH. WHY ARE WARLOCKS SO ANNOYING?!

"Don't try to change the subject," I say, waggling my finger at him. "The point is, what are we going to do?"

"What can we do?" His eyes scan the crowd, landing on Iris, who is laughing on the other side of the room with Kareen. "We just have to wait and see. Maybe she'll forget about it."

"Or the dreams might get clearer. Our faces might come into focus."

"I'm sure that won't happen," Owen says, shaking his head. "The memory will fade with time."

"I hope so. Otherwise, we're going to need to do some more magic."

He frowns at me. "I don't think we can, Morgan, not after everything that went wrong. Remember what we agreed before Christmas. No more magic. It's for the best."

"Don't worry, I promise this term will be different," I say, looking up at him determinedly. "No more magic."

✦ Three ✦

The day before the new term starts, Dora comes over with a big surprise.

"What do you think of my new pet?" she asks eagerly, standing in the doorway with the biggest dog I've ever seen in my life.

"He's wonderful!" I exclaim, opening my arms wide as she closes the front door behind her and lets go of the lead.

The dog bounds forwards, leaping at me with his gigantic paws, sending me flying backwards. Dora clicks her fingers just in time so that a mattress suddenly appears on the floor beneath me, providing a soft landing. Pinning me down, the dog begins to cover my face in slobbery licks.

"His name is Puffin," Dora tells me proudly, as I burst into giggles.

She grabs his lead and pulls him off me so that I can scramble to my feet and stroke his head, his tongue lolling out of his jaws. Dora and Howard are animal lovers and their house next door is not all that different from a zoo. As well as owning plenty of pets, they also foster a lot of rescues, so there's always an amazing variety of animals to welcome you when you walk through their doors and you're never quite sure what to expect. Over the years they've had dogs, cats, pigs, rodents, snakes and a chameleon named Tobias, who they lost for a bit until they found him blending in with Dora's bedside lamp.

Dora's familiar Mac takes the same form whenever he's at home, so Howard thinks that he owns a corgi, too.

"Puffin is lovely," I declare, wrapping my arms around his neck and giving him a cuddle as he slobbers excitedly over my ear. "Where did you find him, Dora?"

"The rescue centre. Apparently his previous owners didn't realize Great Danes get so big," she sighs, rolling her eyes. "I agreed to foster him but then as soon as I met Puffin, I knew he was my dog. Howard couldn't be happier. He's always wanted a big dog."

"He didn't seem that happy this morning when Puffin knocked over the television," Mac comments drily, hiding behind Dora's legs in his corgi form. "Or last night when Puffin stole an entire loaf of bread off the table and ate the whole thing in two bites."

Puffin licks his chops proudly.

"Of course, he does need a little bit of training," Dora says, shooting Mac a look over her shoulder. "But he'll get there. He's extremely intelligent."

Puffin's tongue lolls out of his jaws again and a pool of drool begins to form on the floor.

"He's boisterous," Mac huffs.

"He's magnificent," Merlin says in the form of a chipmunk. He scrabbles up Puffin's leg to sit on his back. "He's the size of a small horse. You could do an awful lot of damage with a dog this big." Merlin grins mischievously at me, rubbing his paws together. "Think of the chaos! *Think of it!*"

"All right, Merlin," I say, raising my eyebrows at him. "Don't encourage any—"

"RELEASE THE HOUND!" Merlin bellows, unclipping the lead from Puffin's collar and holding on to his fur for dear life.

Puffin lurches forwards and lollops into the sitting room, limbs everywhere. Dora and I chase after him as he runs circles around the room. Crashes echo through the house while vases and photo frames go flying, soaring through the air after being swiped from the coffee tables by the ferocious wagging of Puffin's powerful tail.

"What is going on in here?!"

Mum appears in the doorway as Dora and I stand motionless, watching the chaos unfold in front of us. Merlin is still clinging to Puffin's back, calling out, "YOOOHOOOOO!" as he is carried back and forth at great speed.

"This is my new pet, Puffin," Dora explains, wincing at another smash, tiny bits of vase scattering across the carpet. "Isn't he gorgeous?"

"He's really something." Mum puts her hands on her hips and calls out, "Puffin! Sit!"

Puffin digs his paws into the ground, coming to a sudden halt and catapulting Merlin through the air. Just before he slams slap-bang into the middle of the wall, Merlin transforms into a mosquito and flits upwards dizzily.

Puffin trots obediently over to Mum and sits down in front of her.

"Very good," she tells him.

She clicks her fingers and the sitting room magically begins to piece itself back together again: the shards of glass reframing themselves around photos, the bits of vase reshaping themselves and landing neatly on the tables where they were before, the flower stems slotting back into their arrangements. When she's done, the room looks tidier and feels more tranquil than it did before, even with a giant dog panting in the middle of it.

"Let's have some tea," Mum says, gesturing to the sofas. "Sugar, Dora?"

"I won't today, thanks, Aggie," she says, sitting down and making herself comfortable.

Mum clicks her fingers again and three cups of tea come bobbing through the air from the kitchen, landing in our hands as we place ourselves around the room. I settle cross-legged on the floor, Merlin taking the form of a black cat and coming to curl up in my lap.

Puffin is still sitting smartly in front of Mum, awaiting instruction. She clicks her fingers and a large, cosy dog bed appears in the corner of the room alongside a water bowl and a chewy bone.

"You make yourself at home, Puffin," Mum says, nodding to the bed.

He licks her hand gratefully and then trots over to nestle down in the bed, gnawing away happily at his bone.

"I don't know how you do it, Aggie," Dora sighs, watching Puffin fondly as Mac settles at her feet for a snooze, still in his favourite corgi form. "Even animals know that you're the boss."

"It's simply establishing authority." Mum chuckles, taking a seat next to her friend while Helena sits on her shoulder as a butterfly. "You've always been a soft touch and neither your pets nor I would have you any other way."

Dora smiles, putting her tea down and smoothing the crinkles in her bright pink skirt. It's amazing how well Dora and my mum get on, considering how different they are. Stand them next to one another and you'd never guess they were the best of friends. Dora is an explosion of colour, all bows and rainbow patterns, while my mum constantly looks like she's on her way to chair a very important board meeting, even when she's just lounging around the house all day.

With Dora living right next door, it's almost like I have two mums, something I feel very grateful for, especially the times when Mum and I have had a fight. If I need some space, I can just walk a few paces over to Dora's and lounge about there in a big strop and be fed freshly-baked cookies and told I'm wonderful.

Stuff like that means I've never really missed having a dad. I did have one once, but he left when I was a baby and has never been in touch, so I don't know anything about him. I guess you can't miss what you never had.

Mum never talks about my dad. I don't like asking

her too many questions because on the rare occasions that he crops up in conversation, she gets this sad look on her face which she tries to hide from me, but you can see it in her eyes. She doesn't have to say it, but I know from that look that whoever my dad was, he really broke my mum's heart.

I've come up with loads of theories about my dad. I'm pretty sure that whoever he is, he's awesome. That's because there's no way my mum would ever fall for anyone lame, and then still be heartbroken about him all these years later. No, he has to be someone INCREDIBLE, probably with a really important job, the kind that forces you away from your family for the good of the world.

When I was little I thought maybe he was an astronaut and had been orbiting the Earth all this time, or was on a groundbreaking mission to a different planet, light years away. What a stupid, unrealistic theory. Come on. An astronaut? So childish.

Now that I'm older, I have a much more sensible theory.

It's obvious that my dad is a spy.

Why else would he need to *completely* disappear? He is deep undercover somewhere and any contact with his daughter would be highly dangerous. It's a great sacrifice, but he must be the type that puts his country first, like James Bond, and I respect that. No wonder my mum gets so upset when she thinks about him. He's clearly brave and courageous and full of integrity. Who could live up to a guy like that?

Sometimes I wonder if one day, when he's done saving the world, I'll get to meet him.

I hope so.

"How was the New Year's Eve party, Morgan?" Dora asks eagerly, rubbing her hands together and disturbing my train of thought.

"It was ... uh ... fine," I say simply, before taking a sip of tea.

"That's all I've managed to get out of her," Mum tells Dora. "It can't have gone badly, though. She stayed quite a while."

"Very impressive!" Dora exclaims, prompting me to roll my eyes.

"Why is that so surprising?" I huff, putting my mug down and absent-mindedly stroking Merlin, his tail swishing contentedly.

"Only because we had to force you out the house and you kept telling us that you'd need picking up within ten minutes," Mum points out, smirking at me. "All your dramatic goings-on about how *everyone* at school hates you and you don't have *any* friends. But, admit it, you had a wonderful time at the party, just like we predicted."

"I wouldn't describe it as wonderful," I mutter. "It was . . . fine."

Mum and Dora chuckle, shaking their heads at me before moving the conversation on to Mum's work as Dora asks her about the big new project she's been working on.

The truth is, I did have a good time at the party, but mainly thanks to Owen and Iris. Without them, I really would have had to escape within ten minutes because it was obvious no one else wanted me there.

Owen and I had to stop talking about magic sharpish when Iris came over to us, and then because she was there, Felix came skulking back, forced to put up with my company, and before long a few people were crowded into our corner and I was able to start enjoying myself, joining conversations and acting like a normal person at a party.

Merlin also behaved himself, staying hidden and taking the opportunity to have a snooze, curled up on my shoulder in the form of a caterpillar.

So, yes, most of it was fun, BUT I also managed to completely RUIN the party.

Thankfully, only Owen and I know what *really* happened, but still.

It was during the fireworks, when we were all standing in Iris's garden admiring the colourful display of lights exploding above us, brightening the night sky. Owen leaned over and whispered in my ear something about how the no-magic rule technically starts when we're back at school for the new term.

"So?"

"So," he'd said, "maybe you could make these fireworks even better for us all."

It's a simple piece of magic. I've done a fireworks spell loads of times.

I clicked my fingers and the fireworks got bigger and better, the most spectacular fireworks for miles. There were plenty of gasps, "oooooohs" and "aaaaaaaahs" from the crowd as everyone's eyes widened in amazement at the display.

Then Owen had leaned in towards my ear again and said, "Not bad for a witch."

And I'd turned to face him so I could make a snide comment about warlocks, but he was standing so close to me that my brain got all jumbled and I felt this weird jolt as I looked up into his eyes.

Suddenly, there was a loud bang that made us jump, before a series of similar sounds followed. The fireworks had got completely out of control and were exploding like crazy, zipping and whizzing through the sky in all directions. Everyone began screaming and running back towards the house as the fireworks swooped low to the ground, going off all around us.

"Morgan!" Owen had yelled, his hands covering his ears as he ducked low to the floor. "What have you done?"

I'd flattened myself on the grass as a firework had soared towards us, narrowly missing my head before looping upwards and exploding just above the roof tiles.

"You need to focus!" Merlin had instructed into my ear. "Morgan! Focus!"

Shutting out the screams and yells of my classmates as they ran for dear life, ducking behind trees and hedges and flinging themselves back through the doors of the house, I'd closed my eyes and taken a deep breath in, focusing on my calm and serene magic.

I'd clicked my fingers and the fireworks had come to a stop.

"Well done," Merlin had said. "Now, perhaps do a bit of damage control."

While the other partygoers and Iris's family breathed a sigh of relief and began to get to their feet, I'd clicked my fingers quickly and the scorch marks littering Iris's garden disappeared under the cover of darkness, while the roof tiles moved back into position and the smoke clouding us evaporated.

Apart from the terrified looks on everyone's faces, you'd never have guessed what had just happened.

"Well, I guess we've proved our point," Owen had said, coming over and wiping the mud off his jeans. "We really should stick to the no-magic agreement."

Ever since that happened, I've tried to work out how it went so badly.

"It's because I lost focus," I'd said to Merlin the other day when we'd been talking about it. "I need to concentrate when I perform magic. A clear head is so important."

"Hmm," Merlin had said, his cat eyes flashing at me. "I wonder what made you lose control."

"It should have been a really simple spell," I'd said grumpily, annoyed at myself for being so rubbish. "I need to practise more."

"Interesting, though," Merlin had said.

"What is?"

"Normally when witches lose control, the magic fades or dims. It shuts down." He'd swished his tail, watching me curiously. "When *you* lose control, your magic gets more powerful."

"Brilliant, thanks, Merlin," I'd said sarcastically,

narrowing my eyes at him. "Go ahead and point out how much more of a freak I am. I get it, OK? I'm strange."

He hadn't answered but stayed watching me for a while, which freaked me out a bit. I hope he's not thinking of snitching on me to Mum. He wouldn't do that.

I don't think.

"Are you excited to get back to school, Morgan?" Dora asks. "Got your witch backpack ready?"

"It's packed full of my boring textbooks," I inform her. "I'm just glad there aren't any talent shows I need to worry about this term. My plan is to work hard, keep my head down, blend in with the crowd and not get in anybody's way."

"Oh, Morgan, you're much too special," Dora says, grinning at me. "You couldn't blend in if you tried."

CHAPTER

✦ Four ✦

The first day of a new term is a chance for a fresh start.

I keep telling myself that over and over as I wave goodbye to Mum and head through the school gates, fiddling nervously with the necklace she gave me for my birthday last year. It starts drizzling as I make my way towards the main school building and by the time I'm heading up the steps, it's beginning to pour. I push through the door and am instantly hit by a wave of noise, as students chat enthusiastically on their way down the corridor, filling each other in on their holidays. Riddle House is a very big school and, having been home-schooled all my life, I still find the number of students here very overwhelming. I duck as a random football goes flying down the hall, bouncing off someone's head and causing an outburst of giggles.

Keeping myself out of everyone's way, I eventually make it to my locker and start sorting out what books I'll need. An older boy knocks into my shoulder and doesn't bother to apologize as he continues to barge down the corridor.

"Maybe you're right and you do need to practise some simple spells," Merlin mumbles grumpily in his spider form, sitting on my shoulder and glaring at the back of the boy who barrelled into us. "May I suggest turning that young man into a toad?"

"I'll consider it."

"Next time we see him, I'll take the form of a panther and have a little nibble on his arm."

"I'd really rather you didn't," I sigh, sliding my history book into my backpack. "Remember how well it turned out when you made an appearance to my schoolmates last term?"

Merlin chuckles to himself. "It was a lot of fun. You should have seen Felix's face when he saw a tarantula giving him a little wave."

"I *did* see Felix's face," I remind him through gritted teeth. "And then everyone thought I was a freak for bringing a pet spider to school."

"So, it's a no to the panther?"

"It's a strong no."

"You're no fun," Merlin huffs. "If only I'd been the familiar of a truly dangerous and evil witch. Life would have been so interesting."

I roll my eyes, refusing to take Merlin's bait. He often slides in comments like these, hoping to rile me up, but it's pointless. Witches don't get to choose the familiar they are landed with for life, and familiars don't get to pick their witch. Merlin and I are stuck with each other, no matter what.

It's all very depressing.

"Hey, Morgan!" Owen appears at my side, grinning as he runs a hand through his dark, scruffy hair. "Ready for the first day of school?"

"Ready as I'll ever be," I say, flinching as someone else zooms past, almost knocking into me. "Are you heading to assembly?"

"Yeah, let's go," he says. I slam my locker shut and fall into step with him. "So, you didn't reply to my messages," he continues. "Are we going to talk about what happened at the party?"

He shoots me a very annoying grin. I narrow my eyes at him.

"Nothing happened."

"You almost burned down Iris's house."

"Could you keep your voice down?" I hiss, glancing

around. "And I did NOT burn down her house. I was completely in control of the situation."

"HA!" He shakes his head. "Are you joking? Everyone had to run for cover."

"Which is exactly what I intended. You asked for a big show and I delivered."

"You almost killed me and several of our school friends."

"You are so dramatic. You did not almost die because a couple of tiny fireworks went a bit berserk."

"Those tiny fireworks trended on Twitter," he comments, trying to stifle a laugh. "Iris's neighbour called the police."

I grimace.

"Don't worry about it, though, nobody knows it was your fault," Owen says, noticing my reaction.

"Thank goodness." I let out a long sigh. "I don't know how it happened; I should have been able to do a fireworks spell."

Owen shrugs. "I wouldn't feel bad about it. Happens all the time with witches."

"*Excuse me?*" I stop him as we get to the double doors leading to the assembly hall. "What's that supposed to mean?"

"Nothing! It's just, you know, a typical witch trait,"

he whispers, moving away from the noisy crowd jostling through the doors. "I don't mean it personally."

"What's a typical witch trait?"

The corners of his mouth twitch as he tries not to smile. "Attempting a spell you haven't quite mastered yet."

My jaw drops to the floor. "WHAT?"

"Please," Merlin whispers into my ear, "*please* let me turn into a lion and bite off his head. It would be so *easy*."

"Hey, Merlin," Owen says, unbothered by the spider fangs being bared at him. "How are you?"

"Don't talk to my familiar," I hiss, jabbing my finger at him. "How DARE you say that about witches?! Take it back!"

"Oh, come on, Morgan." He chuckles, clearly enjoying that he's succeeding in winding me up. "You have to admit that this happens all the time. A witch gets a bit carried away, everything goes wrong, and then it's left to us warlocks to wipe everyone's memories. It's not a bad thing, it just happens. I guess warlocks are a bit more controlled and steady. We like to make sure our magic is perfect before we test it out."

"Witches always do perfect magic!"

"Like the fireworks spell?"

"That was a one-off. And warlocks are much worse than witches when it comes to spells going wrong. The other day, the Chief Warlock had to ask my mum to sort out a HUGE disaster due to a warlock drinking a potion that he hoped would turn him into a genie. Instead, he turned himself into a giant walking lamp, stomping round town! And what about your memory-loss potion with Iris, huh? That's clearly not perfect!"

"You forced me to make that. I told you I hadn't done it properly before."

"You were the one who encouraged me to do the fireworks!"

"I know and I'm sorry. You should have said if you weren't ready to do that kind of magic. Look, I'm not saying witches aren't brilliant, because . . . you *are* in your own way, I guess," he admits, looking slightly pained by his words. "I'm just saying it would be better to stick to simple spells that you've practised and that you're confident in. And that don't almost take out your entire class."

"I am confident in that spell. You're WRONG. And you're the most irritating person on the planet!"

Owen holds his hands up, sighing. "OK, I'll drop it. Can we go into assembly now? Or do you want us to be late and get landed with detention on our first day?"

"I can do more than just simple spells," I tell him, as he holds open the door for me and we go into the bustling hall. "I'll prove it."

"What?" He frowns at me. "Morgan, what do you mean?"

"You'll see," I say with a smirk, taking my seat.

He sits down next to me, looking nervous. "Morgan, you wouldn't do anything now, right?"

YOU BET I WOULD, OWEN. YOU BET I WOULD.

"Of course not," I whisper back, giving him a sweet, innocent smile. "Witches never get carried away."

I'M ABOUT TO GET VERY CARRIED AWAY.

"Good morning, everyone!" Mr Hopkins, our headmaster, comes striding confidently up on to the stage and the hall falls silent. "Welcome back to the new term; I hope you all had a wonderful holiday. I'm sure you're all dying to get to your lessons – " there's a collective groan – "so I won't keep you long, but I have a few notices to read out..."

As gently and quietly as possible, I concentrate on my SIMPLE spell and click my fingers.

Owen hears the sound and turns to look at me, his eyes wide with horror.

"The first announcement," Mr Hopkins continues, "is that we are joined by a new science teacher this term, so I'd like us all to give a big welcome to—"

"OINK! OINK! OINK!"

Mr Hopkins is rudely interrupted by Owen doing

a very loud pig snort. Owen clasps his hands over his mouth as the auditorium erupts into giggles.

"Mr Blaze!" Miss Campbell, the history teacher, swivels round in her seat a row in front of us to face Owen. "What do you think you're doing?"

"Sorry!" he says, sliding down in his seat, glaring at me.

"Uh, well, I'm not sure what that was about," Mr Hopkins says, clearing his throat and craning his neck to give Owen a warning look across the sea of faces, "but if I may continue. Please can we all give a warm welcome to our new science teacher, Miss Kelly."

There's a round of applause and a woman at the front of the room stands up awkwardly, gives us a wave and then sits back down.

"The second notice is regarding the school trip that's being organized for next term. I appreciate that seems a while away, but—"

"QUACK! QUACK! QUACK!"

Owen's duck impression causes an explosion of laughter as everyone looks in our direction.

"*OWEN!*" Miss Campbell says, turning round again and scowling at him. "I don't know why you're acting so out of character, but one more peep from you and you'll get detention! Is that clear?"

Owen nods, his lips clamped together. When she's

swivelled back and as Mr Hopkins attempts to quieten his audience once again, Owen turns to me with a thunderous expression.

"OK, you've proved your point. Now, can you *please* make it stop?"

"Yes," I whisper, Merlin sniggering away with delight on my shoulder. "If you admit that witches are better than warlocks."

"Never."

"Suit yourself."

"As I was saying," Mr Hopkins growls, clapping his hands loudly to get everyone's attention, "I appreciate it's early to start thinking about the summer half-term trip, but Mrs Fernley, who is organizing it, would like to know a rough idea of numbers. And the last notice today is—"

"BAAAAAAAAAAAA! BAAAAAAAAAAAAAAA! BAAAAAAAAAAA!"

I lose it as Owen bleats away enthusiastically, laughing so hard that tears start rolling down my cheeks. I'm not the only one. People are howling with laughter and even applauding him, standing up to get a better look at the student causing all this chaos.

"THAT'S IT!" Mr Hopkins calls out over the noise. "Owen Blaze, you have landed yourself in detention for the week!"

"BAAAAAAAAAAA!"

"Two weeks!" Mr Hopkins cries, his face flushed red with indignation.

"Fine!" Owen squeaks, so low down in his chair that he's practically on the floor. "Witches are better!"

I nod smugly and click my fingers, ending the spell. I did notice that his fingers were crossed when he said it, but I decide that I've punished him enough.

Now, he'll think twice before insulting witches. I know I promised Mum I wouldn't use magic again at school, but if she knew the reason behind this spell, she'd be in full support. Warlocks are always in great need of being brought down a few pegs. And, frankly, this morning proves that witches are definitely better – I can conjure magic whenever I like. It's not like Owen can get his revenge right now, he'd have to sneak off, get his cauldron and spend ages creating a potion before finding a way for me to drink it. I can simply click my fingers and embarrass him.

See? Warlocks suck.

"All right, that's enough!" Mr Hopkins yells out as the auditorium titters at Owen's performance. "Everyone quiet down! I've got one very important final announcement and then you can disappear."

He rubs his forehead, waiting for silence, already

looking as though he needs another holiday. Owen glares daggers at me and every now and then mutters something under his breath about overreactions. When the audience is suitably quiet, and with one last withering look in Owen's direction, Mr Hopkins begins to speak again.

"I have some very exciting news. This term, Riddle House will be taking part in the inter-school quiz competition, SCHOOL CHALLENGE! As some of you may already know, the competition focuses on one region at a time with two schools competing against each other in a general knowledge quiz. We will be taking on Woodvale School."

Boos echo around the assembly hall and Mr Hopkins chuckles.

"Yes, our local rivals! No match for Riddle House. There are four rounds, each more difficult than the last, and the team that scores the most points across all the rounds at the end of the final wins. The Riddle House team will also have the chance to be TV stars as the last round of the quiz will be televised! And when the winner has been announced, there will be a big school dance, kindly hosted by Woodvale, to celebrate our friendly rivalry and, no doubt, that we are the champions!"

The announcement is met with cheers and whoops,

as well as a ripple of excited gasps and chatter about the prospect of the dance.

"The teams will be made up of volunteers from Years Nine and Ten," Mr Hopkins goes on, pleased with the enthusiastic reaction. "Please let your form teacher know if you would like to be considered by the end of tomorrow."

CHAPTER

✦ Five ✦

"If we're on the team for the quiz, then we'll be famous, right?" Felix muses the following morning, bouncing a tennis ball against the classroom wall.

"Not exactly." Iris snorts, sitting on top of her desk, swinging her legs. "It's not going to be a big prime-time television show. I've never heard of it."

"Yeah, but it's still on TV," Felix reasons. "Chances are, a talent agent might be watching and sign me up afterwards."

"And what talent will the agent be signing you up for, Felix?" Lucy asks, not bothering to look up from her phone. "The ability to be the biggest idiot in every room?"

"Maybe it will be his catching skills," Owen says with

a smile, as Felix misses the tennis ball and Owen reaches out in time to catch it going over his head.

"I've got plenty of talents," Felix says, ignoring everyone's giggles and snatching the ball back from Owen. "And the world will see that when I make the quiz team and become a big TV star."

I stay quiet, pleased that I get to be a part of this conversation because Owen and Iris are here. The bell hasn't rung for the first lesson yet, but it's raining again so everyone's hanging out in their classrooms. I'm not sure Owen has completely forgiven me for yesterday's assembly, not that I need forgiving. As I pointedly told him when he was yelling at me afterwards, he shouldn't have insulted me.

"You insult warlocks all the time!" he'd argued.

"Yes, but that is justified," I'd said, crossing my arms. "Warlocks are stupid."

"I can't believe I now have detention because of you using magic again. You said you wouldn't this term!"

"And I won't!" I'd declared. "From now on. The first day doesn't count."

He'd grumbled something inaudible, but I think he could tell I meant it. I fully intend not to use magic again this term, it was just that one time. It was a harmless bit of fun. Owen needs to find his sense of humour.

And anyway, Owen had received many compliments from classmates about his versatile range of animal impressions. If anything, he should be THANKING ME.

"Are you volunteering for the quiz show, Iris?" Felix asks, as always trying to get her attention.

She shakes her head. "No, I've got too much on this term. I want to put my full focus on the dance team. It's going to be taking up a lot of my time."

"Fair enough," Felix says, flinging the tennis ball at the wall. "Lucy?"

"Absolutely," she says, sitting up straight and flicking her hair behind her shoulders. "I plan on being team captain."

"No chance," Felix says. "Sorry, but that title has already been taken."

"What makes you think you'd be made captain over me?"

"I have great leadership skills." He shrugs. "Everyone tells me that all the time. You're not really captain material."

"Ignore him, Lucy," Iris says, elbowing Felix in the ribs. "I think you'd make an excellent captain of the team."

"Thanks." Lucy smiles up at her best friend.

"What about you, Morgan?" Iris asks.

"Huh?" I blurt out, startled by the attention.

Felix smirks. "I think that reaction tells us enough. She can't even hold a conversation, let alone survive a quiz show."

"Shut up, Felix," Iris sighs tiredly. "I was talking to Morgan."

"Felix is right," I say, my face growing hot as the group watches me. "I'm not one for public speaking and I'm not very good at general knowledge, so I really can't think of anything worse than being in the quiz team."

"I think you'd be good at it," Iris says thoughtfully.

"She'd absolutely hate all the attention," Owen comments, swooping in front of Felix to catch the tennis ball under his nose.

"And how would we know that she'd show up on the day?" Felix sneers, his eyes flashing at me. "You have a reputation for dropping out of shows at the last minute, don't you?"

"Good one," I say, hearing Merlin sigh under my shirt collar. "The stage clearly isn't my calling, so I'll be steering clear of it. As Owen said, I'd be useless anyway."

"I didn't say that, I said you'd hate the attention," Owen points out stubbornly. "Iris is right. You might be good at something like that if you had the confidence to try."

"Does anyone want a cookie?" Kareen suddenly appears next to us, holding out a box of delicious-smelling biscuits. "I made them last night and was meant to save them for lunch but I'm already hungry."

"YES," Felix says, grabbing two from the box and stuffing them in his mouth. "What a breakfast!"

"Gross, Felix," Lucy says, as Felix sprays crumbs everywhere. "And save some for everyone else. Thanks, Kareen."

A crowd forms around Kareen, but I hold back, aware that she's probably offering them to her friends, a group in which I definitely don't belong.

"Yeah, Felix, give us all a chance," Owen says, before coming over to where I'm sitting and holding out a chocolate chip cookie for me. "I'd take it now before Felix eats the whole lot."

"I wouldn't eat *all* of them," Felix retorts through a mouthful of biscuit, overhearing Owen's comment.

"Thanks," I say quietly, smiling up at Owen and taking a bite.

I thank Kareen along with everyone else and we all laugh as Felix reaches for another one and Kareen swiftly moves the box out of his reach. The bell goes and the class reluctantly take their seats. Joe, the boy who is forced to sit next to me, makes his way to our desk and slumps into his chair, dropping his bag on the floor, not bothering to say hi. We almost became friends last year when he thought I might be able to teach him how to breakdance, but yesterday he barely spoke a word to me, so I guess he's back to having the same low opinion of me as everyone else has.

"I hate Felix," Merlin whispers, in the form of a ladybird, sat on top of my ear beneath my hair.

I nod in agreement.

"Did you know you have quite hairy ears?" Merlin suddenly comments. "I've only just noticed."

"Shush," I hiss.

"I didn't say anything," Joe replies, turning to me with an insulted expression.

"Sorry, I wasn't talking to you," I say hurriedly. "I was talking to ... me. Telling my brain to shush. You know how it is."

Joe stares at me, clearly not knowing at all how it is and wishing he was sitting next to someone else.

"Morning, class!" Miss Campbell trills, swanning into the room with a coffee.

We all mumble good morning back and wait for her to get the register ready.

Suddenly, I start to feel a bit weird. I shift in my seat, trying to ignore a warm, tingling sensation beginning to grow in my stomach. It spreads throughout my body, running down my arms and legs, like pins and needles but a good version.

I feel *fantastic*.

Wow. You know what? I am ready for anything, today! I could tackle the biggest challenge that comes my way! I've never been excited to do classwork before but, right now, I am SUPER eager to get started. I can't control it; I'm on the edge of my seat, my hands clinging to the edges as though if I let go, I might soar upwards and hit my head on the ceiling.

Having been determined to ignore me after our initial conversation, Joe is now staring wide-eyed at me as I practically bounce up and down in my seat with enthusiasm.

"You OK?" he whispers to me nervously, as Miss Campbell begins the register.

"Joe, I am GREAT. I am FABULOUS. I am EXCITED. Are you, Joe?! What a wonderful moment! What an amazing day! What a brilliant school! I am so excited for today! Are you, Joe? Are you excited for today?"

He blinks at me. "Um. No."

"Morgan Charmley?" Miss Campbell calls out, looking up from her list.

"HERE!" I cry, leaping to my feet and sticking

53

my hand in the air. "I AM AT SCHOOL, MISS CAMPBELL, AND I AM SO ENTHUSIASTIC TO BE HERE!"

"Oh! Good," Miss Campbell says, shocked at my response.

I sink back into my seat, still jittery with excitement about the register, indifferent to the rest of the class laughing at me. I hear Felix mutter "freak" and it doesn't faze me one bit, because who cares? I am ready to learn! I am ready to smile! I am ready to talk to my fellow students! I am ready to eat lunch at lunchtime! I CAN'T WAIT FOR THE REST OF THE DAY!

"Morgan, what's going on?" Merlin says urgently into my ear.

"No idea! Which is great!"

"No, it's not. Why would you suddenly..." He trails off and then I hear him groan. "Owen."

"What?"

"The cookie," he sighs, transforming into a spider and scuttling down from my ear to my shoulder. "He must have put a potion on it."

"No way! Why would he—"

"OK, everyone, time for you to volunteer for School Challenge!" Miss Campbell announces. "This is an amazing opportunity—"

"IT'S AN AMAZING OPPORTUNITY!" I echo, barely able to contain my excitement.

"Yes, thank you, Morgan," Miss Campbell says, giving me a strange look. "I'm hoping there will be a few volunteers from this class for us to consider for the team. So without further ado . . ."

"*Uh-oh,*" Merlin sighs. "Here we go."

". . . do I have any volunteers for the school quiz team?"

"MEEEEEEEEEEEEEEEEEE!" I cry at the top of my lungs, leaping up to stand on my chair and waving my arms madly about my head. "ME! I VOLUNTEER!"

"My goodness." Miss Campbell laughs, along with the rest of the class. "I am delighted with such enthusiasm. Very well, Morgan, I shall pop your name down on the list."

"WONDERFUL!" I say, clapping my hands. "How brilliant!"

"You can sit down now," she prompts.

I take my seat and hold up my hand for Joe to high-five. He looks terrified and obliges. I know I said earlier that I would hate being on the quiz team, but hey! Things change! I AM SO EXCITED!

I spot Owen watching me from the other side of the room and I smile at him, giving him a big wave because he's my friend and it is so GREAT to have friends.

He waves back, a grin spreading across his face.

CHAPTER

✦ Six ✦

What have I done?

WHAT HAVE I DONE?

The potion wears off after about an hour and the truth of what's just happened suddenly begins to creep in. I have volunteered for the school quiz team. I hate speaking in front of audiences. I am terrible at general knowledge. I do not want to go on TV.

I am going to *kill* Owen Blaze.

"You have to give it to him, it's an impressive bit of magic," Merlin says in the form of a raven, sitting on the windowsill.

I've escaped into the girls' toilets in between classes and, since there's no one else in here for the time being, Merlin has taken the opportunity to spread his wings.

"It's not impressive at all," I huff, washing my hands and shuddering, my fingers tingling as the potion continues to wear off. "It's sabotage!"

"I've always been a fan of a good revenge story."

"Well, then, you'll be pleased to hear I'm already plotting how to get back at him. I can't believe this! All I did was land him in detention for a couple of weeks. He has caused me to volunteer to take part in a show that will be on national television. I'm feeling sweaty just thinking about it."

"Gross."

"Merlin," I sigh, turning to look up at him, "what am I going to do?"

Merlin looks at me with his beady raven eyes. "Do you really need a spirit guide to tell you how to handle getting out of a school activity? Tell Miss Campbell that you made a mistake and you don't want to volunteer."

"It looks a bit strange, though, doesn't it? To go from being that enthusiastic to dropping out in the space of an hour?"

"Do you want to get out of it or not?" Merlin huffs, pointing his beak at me. "The only other option you have is to fake a serious illness on the day."

"I can't do that," I say, pushing my hair behind my ears. "I already have a reputation for ruining things at the last minute. You're right, the sooner I talk to her, the better. Let's go."

He swoops down and lands on my shoulder, transforming into an earwig and crawling into his usual spot beneath my collar. I take a deep breath and with my chin up, I open the bathroom door and march back to Miss Campbell's classroom, determined not to let Owen Blaze ruin my day.

"Miss Campbell," I say, sidling up to her desk as she prepares for her next lesson, "can I please have a word?"

She smiles up at me before checking her watch. "Sure, there's five minutes until the bell goes, Morgan. How can I help?"

"Um. It's . . . it's about the quiz."

"Yes." She beams at me. "I think it's simply wonderful that you've volunteered, Morgan. I really couldn't be happier. I'm going to highly recommend you for the team."

"Eh?" I say, stunned.

"Intelligent response," Merlin quietly sighs.

"Last term, I always felt like you were holding back," Miss Campbell continues. "It took a while for you to come out of your shell in my history lessons, but then you showed me just what you could do with all those fantastic papers you handed in. When you put your mind to it and let yourself enjoy the work, you're really quite outstanding."

58

Ah. What I can't point out here is that I was cheating last term. I used magic to help me get ahead with classwork. Not my finest moment.

"That's nice of you to say, but—"

"The quiz team needs someone like you! I think it will be a brilliant way for you to find your confidence." She tilts her head at me sympathetically. "I know you had a bit of a rough time at the end of last term, but I think you'll find this quiz is the perfect opportunity to show everyone what you're about. You have such potential and I'm so happy that you've taken the step to put yourself out there and go for it. You're an inspiration!"

"I'm ... no ... uh ... I'm not—"

She stands up, puts a hand on my shoulder and says in a quiet, sincere manner, "I'm proud of you, Morgan."

I swallow the lump in my throat as she looks me right in the eye.

"What did you want to ask me?" she says brightly as the bell rings for the next class, looking over my shoulder at the students beginning to troop into her classroom. "You don't need to worry about volunteering formally, if that's what you're asking. I will let Mr Hopkins know who's keen."

I nod in a daze. "Right. Great."

"Off you go, then. You're going to be late."

Before I can get my brain to start working properly again, she's ushered me out of the classroom and into the corridor.

"That went well." Merlin sniggers.

"What was I supposed to do?" I hiss at him, burying my head in my hands. "She was saying such nice stuff! I couldn't drop out after she called me an inspiration for volunteering!"

"You're going to go through with it then?"

"No, course not," I snap. "I'll speak to her again later and explain. I have to stand my ground and not be taken in by her compliments. And in the meantime – " I clench my fists angrily – "I need to have a word with a certain warlock."

Owen isn't sorry. Not one bit. He finds it very amusing that I didn't notice him sprinkling a little "enthusiasm potion" on to my cookie, something he'd concocted the night before in the hope of timing it right so that I'd sign up to the quiz competition.

"When Kareen came in with cookies, I couldn't have asked for a better opportunity," he'd said, rubbing his hands together. "You never would have accepted any baked goods from me knowing I was out for revenge."

It's been a very stressful week and his smug attitude

hasn't helped at all. When I first confronted him about it and told him off, he just went, "Don't mess with warlocks, then." And do you know what else he did? *Shrugged*. Shrugged! Like it was nothing. I attempted to keep my voice VERY CALM as I pointed out that I was now in a very difficult situation because I'd have to let down my classmates once again, but he told me I was making a big deal out of nothing and I might not be picked for the team anyway.

"I may have even done you a favour, Morgan," he'd said breezily. "Volunteering makes you look good, and if you don't get picked for the team then it's a win-win situation."

Which is the WORST thing he could have said to me, because, of course, I stupidly believed him and decided not to talk to Miss Campbell again before they posted the list of the final team selection, thinking everything would work out fine. There was no chance they would pick me anyway, and maybe he had a point; volunteering had definitely made me look good in Miss Campbell's eyes.

But then, they'd posted the list and I'd almost had a heart attack.

"Did you bribe them or something, Charmley?" Felix had scoffed when he read my name printed beneath his. "How did you pull this one off?"

"I can't believe *she* got on and I didn't!" Lucy had

stropped, loud enough so I could hear. "She said she didn't want to be on the quiz team!"

"Don't worry, Luce," Felix had said, narrowing his eyes at me. "Charmley will probably drop out and when she does, you can step in."

Speechless, I'd stood in front of the list for a few minutes trying to work out how this could have happened and realizing that it was going to be a hundred times harder trying to get out of the commitment now that it was official for the whole school to see.

After seeing the list, I'd managed to find Miss Campbell and finally tell her that I hadn't meant to volunteer, it was all a big mistake and I wanted out, but she just thought I was being modest.

"You can do this, Morgan," she'd said encouragingly. "Everyone gets scared when they're faced with a challenge, but you have to believe in yourself. You can climb this mountain!"

"But I didn't mean to sign up to climb the mountain in the first place!"

She'd raised her eyebrows. "That's not quite true, is it? I've never seen anyone more enthusiastic to sign up to anything in my life."

"Yes, but it wasn't *me*. I mean, it was me, but it wasn't. If that makes sense."

She'd blinked at me. "Morgan, I'm not going to let you step away from this. You've made the team! You're going to be brilliant."

I've asked her many more times this week and the answer is always the same: she's not letting me drop out.

I inform Owen of this in the park on Saturday. Felix got a new bike for Christmas and decided to try out his "skills" this weekend. Owen extended the group invitation to me and, after much deliberating, I decided I should come along and keep trying to make the group like me again. The only person, aside from Owen, who looked pleased to see me when I arrived in the park was Iris.

Everyone else is pretending I'm not here.

"I don't know what you're so upset about," Owen says, when I come to the end of my rant. "I think it's really nice that Miss Campbell is so behind you."

"That's not the point! You need to help me get out of School Challenge."

"Why should I?"

"Because it's YOU who landed me in this mess in the first place."

We're sitting on a patch of grass a little way off from the rest of the group, who are gathered around the benches next to the bike ramp where Felix is desperately trying to impress everyone. They started off watching him, but now that it's been a while, everyone has got distracted and people aren't paying much attention as he zips from one side of the ramp to the other, unable to pull off many noteworthy tricks.

"What are you so worried about, anyway?" Owen asks curiously. "It's just a quiz. Why don't you give it a try?"

"*Just* a quiz? Owen, this is really important to the school! I'm terrible at quizzes! And I'm useless at public speaking."

"Practice makes perfect."

I snort. "Oh come on. You know as well as I do that this will be a complete disaster unless I find some way of getting out of it."

Owen turns to look at me sharply. "I don't think that."

"Well, you should!"

"Look," he sighs, "I'm not going to say sorry for what I did because you started it with your spell on me in assembly. What I will say, for what it's worth, is that I don't think it is a bad thing that you're on the quiz team. In fact, I think that you could be brilliant."

I stare at him. "You ... you do?"

"Yes," he says, looking at me intently with his dark eyes, "I do."

My mouth suddenly feels very dry as I try to think

of something to say, but he's thrown me off guard by being so nice. I'm used to him teasing me all the time or grumbling about witches; I'm not used to him being so earnest.

"Thanks. I guess," I say eventually.

Felix calls at him to come over and try out the bike, so he gives me a small smile before jumping to his feet and heading over to the ramp. Now that I've been left on my own, Merlin crawls out on to my hand in the form of a beetle.

"We still hate him, remember," he says grumpily.

"*You* hate him," I retort, being sure to turn my head away from the others so they don't think I'm talking to myself. "He's my friend."

"He's a warlock. And he's proven why witches and warlocks shouldn't be friends." Merlin pauses. "You'll end up killing each other."

"Do you have to be so morbid, Merlin?"

"Do you have to be so weird, Morgan?"

I roll my eyes and ignore him, looking back over to Owen, who has put on Felix's helmet and is now on his bike, attempting to master a wheelie.

"That's strange," Merlin suddenly says. "Your necklace."

"What about it?" I ask.

"I thought it was blue when your mum gave it to you

for your birthday," he says, turning into a mosquito so he can fly up and have a closer look.

"It was blue," I say, before peering down at the pendant hanging on the delicate chain round my neck. "I mean, it is blue. Isn't it?"

"No, it's not," Merlin says, hovering next to it, his voice strangely serious. "It's turning grey."

CHAPTER

✦ Seven ✦

"Morgan! MORGAN! MOOOOOOOOOORRRRRRR-
GAAAAAAAAAAAAN!"

I throw open my bedroom door and hurl myself down
the stairs to where I hear Dora shouting in Mum's study.

"What's. . ." I begin, as I get there, but there's no need
for me to finish the question.

I can see instantly what's wrong. Puffin is having the
time of his life bounding around Mum's office and there
are files, paper and books EVERYWHERE. The room
looks as though a tornado has hit it. Dora is desperately
trying to grab Puffin by the collar to slow him down, but
he thinks it's some kind of chasing game and excitedly
dodges around her every time she reaches for him, before
scrabbling around the wall and flying past her again.

I wince as the computer is swept off the desk and crashes to the ground, along with a stack of carefully-ordered files, which scatter across the floor, their contents spilling out and getting mixed up.

"Morgan! Help!" Dora wheezes, lunging unsuccessfully at Puffin.

I wait for the opportune moment and as Dora corners him, I reach out and grab his collar, pulling him towards me. Panting happily, he screeches to a halt, knocking me off balance so that I have to steady myself against the doorframe. I grip his collar tightly as he nuzzles his head into my stomach.

"Hey, Puffin." I laugh, giving him a scratch behind the ear. "Causing chaos again today?"

Puffin responds by sneezing, slobber splattering all over my top.

"I think we need to get one of these," Merlin comments, in the form of a bat, hanging off the light shade and watching Puffin with great admiration.

"I would not recommend it," Mac says, landing on the floor as a hummingbird and transforming into his corgi form. He growls in irritation at Puffin. Puffin doesn't notice.

"Thanks, Morgan," Dora says, out of breath. "He is such a good boy! So much energy. I should take him out in the garden and let him run around a bit. And we already went on a long walk this morning! I love that he's so bouncy!"

"Same," I say, as he licks my hand. "He's wonderful."

"Thanks for helping me catch him," she says, coming over and taking hold of his collar. "He suddenly has these bursts of craziness and won't listen to a word I say. I don't mind, of course, but your mum will be back soon and even though it's an easy fix, I'd rather she didn't witness him destroying all her work."

"You want me to tidy up while you take Puffin out?"

"That would be great," she says, yelping as Puffin eagerly drags her towards the stairs. "Thanks, Morgan!"

I laugh as she lets go of his collar and he bounds down the stairs with Dora and Mac in tow. Even though it's a Sunday, Mum has had to go into work today because of this big new project, so Dora is in charge, so to speak.

I'm a little relieved Mum isn't at home today. I'm worried about her noticing that I've ruined the necklace she gave me. When I came home from the park yesterday, I tried using magic and, when that didn't work, I tried the human method of scrubbing it with a cloth, but the pendant stayed cloudy grey.

I don't know how this has happened because when she gave it to me before the beginning of last term, the pendant was a swirling deep-sea blue, and it's not like it's had that long to age this badly. It's not expensive or anything, but the necklace is very important to the Charmley family. It was gifted to my great grandmother by a warlock who was, naturally, head over heels in love with her. It's been handed down the generations and now it's come to me and I've ruined it. I hate the idea of not wearing it every day but, at the same time, I don't want Mum to see it until I've fixed it. I'll have to make sure the pendant stays hidden under my clothes for now.

Merlin has many theories about why the pendant has changed colour.

"Do you want to hear them?" he asked last night as I climbed into bed.

"It's probably dirt and grime and stuff," I muttered.

"That magic couldn't clean?" Merlin transformed into a pig and sat on my stomach, winding me. "No chance."

"Get off!" I puffed, trying to move him – to no avail.

"I will when you've listened to my theories," he said, pointing a trotter at me.

He then proceeded to list some very creative and ridiculous ideas, but the main one that had him convinced was that this rare, magical necklace reflects the feelings of the witch wearing it.

"So, what would that mean since it's gone from a

sparkling blue to a murky grey?" I asked, twirling the pendant in my fingers. "That I'm feeling . . . grey? I have been a bit down about the quiz and everyone at school not liking me."

Merlin tutted. "You have no imagination."

"What do you think, then?"

He transformed into a black cat and dug his sharp claws into me, his bright yellow eyes flashing with excitement.

"I think you're turning evil."

"Keep dreaming, Merlin." I yawned, checking I'd set my alarm on my phone.

"Any evil ideas you've had lately?" His tail swished eagerly. "Any juicy, flitting thoughts about what it would be like to rule the world? How powerful we could be?"

"Sorry to disappoint you, but my main thoughts have been about how I can make more friends and whether I can pull off a headband."

He gave a heavy sigh. "You'll never make any friends, and no, you can't pull off a headband. You have strange ears."

I thanked him for his input and turned off the light, falling asleep to him grumbling about how familiars shouldn't have to put up with "this teenage nonsense".

Today, my necklace is much the same, so I've tucked

it under my jumper as a precaution, even though Mum isn't in the house.

Scanning across the mess that Puffin has made in the study, I take my time, focus my mind and click my fingers. The magic works instantly. Everything starts picking itself up and floating across the room and back into its rightful place. I lean on the doorframe, smiling as I watch the computer land on the desk, good as new, Mum's edited work notes reorder themselves and slide neatly into the files, and books float up from the floor and begin to slot back on to the bookshelf. One of the best things about being a witch is that you can tidy up without moving a muscle.

As one of Mum's heavy, dog-eared books lifts up, it rotates, preparing to go back on the shelf, and a letter slips out, fluttering to the floor.

I'm about to click my fingers and make it go back into the pages it came from, when I see my name in a sentence at the bottom of the page. I step forward and pick up the letter while the room finishes tidying itself. It is written in black-ink calligraphy on old parchment, which is quite strange in itself. That's a very old magic tradition that no one really sticks to any more. Mum only writes official witch stuff on parchment like this, like when the Witch Council votes on a new magical law. Without opening it properly, I can see the letter is addressed at the top to Mum.

"What is it?" Merlin asks, swooping down and landing on my shoulder. "Looks important."

"Yeah, it does," I say, hesitating as I start to unfold it. "Do you think I should just put it back?"

"When in doubt, don't think, just do and see what happens."

"That seems like terrible life advice."

"What do you expect from me?" Merlin snorts.

I look down at the letter in my hands. "I don't know. Maybe I shouldn't read it. It might be private. Although, I did see my name. . ."

Merlin grins mischievously, showing me his shiny bat fangs. "Open it."

Too curious not to at least read the beginning bit, I unfold the parchment and Merlin and I begin to read.

Dear Aggie,

I'm sorry to do this to you. I'm sorry to leave you and I'm sorry to leave Morgan. I hope you know that I will always love you both, but it is simply impossible for me to stay.

We have both known this for a while, and we have been pretending for too long that the world is not what it is. Aggie, they would destroy us. Rumours are starting to surface. They'd never let us be together. It is better this way. If I leave, our secret is protected. I will return to Bath and then send you details of my movements from there, should you need them.

I hope that, one day, you will forgive me for this and let me see our daughter again. Perhaps, one day, things will change and we won't be magical enemies.

Please tell Morgan our story. Forgive me, Aggie.

Forever yours,
Maverick

I feel numb. I don't move. I can barely breathe. I read the letter again. Then I read it a third time to be sure. My hands begin to shake as I clutch the parchment too tight.

"Morgan," Merlin whispers, horrified, "do you know what this means?"

"Yes," I whisper back, a chill running down my spine. "I *think* my dad is a warlock."

CHAPTER

✦ Eight ✦

I feel sick to my stomach. My head is spinning so much, I have to lean against Mum's desk to steady myself. Feeling a strange urge to cry, I clutch the letter to my chest and then manage to drag my feet out of the study and back to my bedroom. Slamming the door behind me, I stumble towards my bed and sit down, a tear rolling down my cheek before I can stop it. I hate crying.

This letter is wrong. It HAS to be wrong.

The picture it paints doesn't make any sense. This letter makes out that my dad is a *warlock*. That he and my mum were in love with each other, but they had to keep their relationship secret, because they're supposed to be magical enemies. That he left because he wanted to protect us. That he wanted Mum to tell me all this.

ARGH!

I lean forwards and bury my head in my hands, the letter crumpling into my forehead. Merlin has taken the form of a snake and is coiled around my neck, too shocked to make any kind of comment, sarcastic or otherwise.

Maverick.

Mum hates warlocks with a passion. She's raised me to believe that they are inferior magical creatures, who cannot be trusted. It's in our blood to hate them. We are enemies. Mum, as the Great Sorceress, knows this better than anyone. There is absolutely no chance that Mum would ever, EVER fall in love with a warlock. She wouldn't even like a warlock. She'd barely deign to talk to a warlock! The only time she has to do that is when she needs memory-loss potion and, when those days come about, she's always in a terrible mood simply at the idea of having to be in the *presence* of a warlock.

So, in conclusion, looking at the facts, she can't possibly have fallen in love and had a baby with a warlock. It's impossible.

It's much more believable that my dad is a spy. That he didn't know my mum was a witch. That he had to leave us because he was sent on an important MI6 mission somewhere in the world and he is deep undercover so he can't contact us.

That's the correct story. That's the story that makes sense.

But the letter. . .

"He doesn't say explicitly that he's a warlock," I manage to croak. "He doesn't say that. Maybe we've misunderstood."

"What else could he mean by magical enemies?" Merlin hisses, his forked tongue flickering.

"I don't know, maybe he found out she was a witch?" I say desperately. "Maybe he's just a normal guy who happens to be a spy, but discovering she had magical powers was all a bit too much."

"Normal guys don't write letters on parchment with quills, not even spies," Merlin points out. "And he writes about rumours and how 'they' would never let them be together. If he was a normal guy, nobody would mind as long as the secret was safe."

"But, Merlin. . ." I lift my head up to stare at the letter.

"I know," he says quietly.

"This can't be true. It can't be. Maybe this letter is a fake."

"Looks real to me."

"So, Mum has been lying to me all my life? She told me that warlocks are bad, when she fell in love with one! This letter makes her a liar!"

"More importantly, what does this letter make you?"

I frown in confusion as he slithers down from my shoulders to transform into a cat, sitting next to me on the bed.

"What do you mean?"

Merlin sighs, shaking his head. "Morgan, if your father is a warlock and your mother is a witch, *what does that make you?*" He hesitates. "I've never heard of this happening before. Ever."

"What are you saying? That I might not be a witch? That I might be a . . . a *warlock?*" I gasp, horrified.

His tail flicks. "I'm saying that I'm not sure. Maybe you're both."

We sit in silence, Merlin's words hanging in the air.

When Dora comes back in, I say I have too much homework to come downstairs, and hide away in my room for the whole day. I can't bear the idea of speaking to Mum, so pretend to be asleep when she gets home.

The letter stays tightly in my grip the whole night. I don't get any sleep.

I don't understand. I don't understand any of it.

"Merlin, I don't think we should tell Mum that we know," I whisper in the early hours of the morning.

"Fine by me," he mumbles, curled up on my pillow as a white-haired rat.

He also hasn't slept much, spending most of the night airing his frustrations at the idea that he might be the familiar to someone who is part-warlock.

I'm not ready to talk to Mum about this yet. I may have got this all wrong, but it seems unlikely. I've read the letter a hundred times since I found it and I can't think of any other explanation than my dad is a warlock and he left so that Mum wouldn't become a complete outcast of the witch community.

I get up and ready for school hours early, as I can't lie awake any longer. Mum normally drives me to school on her way into work, but there is a way of getting there by bus. That seems better than speaking to her. I'm not sure I can look at her right now.

How could she keep this from me?

I sling my school bag over my shoulder, tiptoeing out of my bedroom and down the stairs. Merlin acts as lookout in the form of a moth, flitting about by my ear and making sure Mum doesn't emerge from her room without me knowing. I leave a note on the kitchen table to say I've gone in early for a quiz meeting and I didn't want to wake her after she had such a hard day at work yesterday. I may be furious with her, but I also don't want her to worry or be on my case, panicking about where I am. This way I can get some space without her realizing that's what I'm doing.

"Merlin, stop looking at me like that," I sigh, waiting at the bus stop on an eerily quiet road.

He's in the form of a cat, sitting next to me on the bench, and every time I glance his way I catch him staring at me, his eyes narrowed into slits.

"I'm not looking at you in any way," he protests.

"Yes, you are. I'm a witch, OK? I've been thinking about it all night and only witches can click their fingers to create magic. Warlocks can't do that. Case closed."

He stays silent.

When the bus appears at the top of the road, he quickly transforms into a stag beetle and scuttles up my sleeve. Thankfully, by the time I get out near the school, the gates are open and the main building has been unlocked, but I still have at least an hour before anyone will start showing up. I sort out the books I need from my locker and head to my form room, enjoying the echo of my footsteps down the empty corridor.

"What am I going to do, Merlin?" I ask, throwing my bag down at my desk and going to stand by the window, looking out over the school grounds. "Should I try to find him?"

Merlin appears at my feet in the form of a fox. "Maverick?"

I nod.

"Why would you want to do that?"

"Because he's my dad."

"He's a warlock."

"We don't know that for certain."

"Yes, we do. There's no other explanation."

"He knows that I exist. He's probably tried to contact me, but Mum's never let him."

"For good reason."

"You think I should just forget about it then?" I say, throwing my arms up in exasperation. "I should pretend that we never saw the letter?"

"I wish we never had," Merlin comments. He gives me a sympathetic look, something I'm not used to from him. "We should think about it for a bit."

"I feel so ... confused," I say, leaning forward and resting my forehead on the glass of the window. "How am I supposed to concentrate at school today?"

"I could transform into a crocodile or a lion and prowl the school," he suggests, brightening at the idea. "They'd have to cancel it for the day."

"Then where would I go? Back home?" I move from the window and slump down into my seat. "It's better to have an excuse to stay away. Keep my mind busy, I guess."

Merlin hops on to my desk as a black cat, looking hopeful. "At least let me cheer us up by playing some pranks on Felix today?"

I groan at the sound of Felix's name, lying forward across the desk and burying my head in my arms.

"Is that a yes or a no?" Merlin asks. "I have some excellent, gruesome ideas. How do you think he feels about pythons? Specifically, pythons slithering up his leg?"

"You just reminded me," I say, my voice muffled by my sleeve, "we have the quiz team meeting at lunchtime today. It's going to be a DISASTER."

Merlin lets out a long, weary sigh. "What's new?"

"CHARMLEY!"

Felix's yell jolts me from my thoughts about Mum and Maverick. My dad, Maverick.

My dad.

"You're doing it again!" Felix cries, towering over me. "I can see your eyes all glazed over! I need you to FOCUS."

"Sorry, sorry," I say hurriedly. "I'm ... I'm a bit tired today."

"No kidding," he huffs, stalking away from me to the front of the classroom where he's been pacing back and forth for the past fifteen minutes, bossily telling everyone how we're going to win this quiz.

It seems at odds with the Felix I'm used to, who

is always messing about in class and never really concentrating on what the teacher is saying. Although, he does love being centre of attention and he's the sort of person who'd do anything to be on TV.

There are five of us on the team: Jacob and Ivy from Year 10; Felix, Holly and myself from Year 9.

Before we even get started, it's obvious that I am by far the weakest link on the team. Holly is very smart, one of the smartest in our year – the only other person who might match her is Jenny from our class. Jenny didn't volunteer though because she already has so many extra-curricular activities and extra classes that she's taking. Jacob and Ivy are also very clever, and Felix would get much better grades if he bothered to put some effort into his schoolwork. I, on the other hand, do not achieve the best grades AND I try as hard as I can.

As Jacob and Ivy are relatively shy, Felix has appointed himself as leader of the team, much to Holly's irritation. I've spent most of our first meeting in another world and Felix is taking great pleasure in having the perfect excuse to tell me off.

"You shouldn't have volunteered if you can't take the pressure, Charmley," Felix says, running a hand through his hair. "You're going to ruin this for everyone. I can't believe you got picked for the team."

"Me neither," I agree, much to the surprise of everyone in the room.

"We don't have long until the first round. We need to swot up on our subjects, play to our strengths," Felix declares. "Now, we're all in this together, so I expect all of us to pull our weight and brush up on general knowledge. I don't want to be humiliated on national TV. It would be good to get an idea of what our individual strengths are. Let's work out what everyone is best at, shall we? I'll go first. I'm very good at sport, so that's going to be my area of expertise."

"I'm not bad at geography," Jacob offers, doodling on his notepad.

"My favourite subject is English, so I'll be sure to practise plenty of literature questions," Ivy says excitedly.

"I'll head up the science questions, then," Holly says happily. "I'm good at science."

"Is anyone keen on music? Those questions pop up a lot in quizzes," Jacob points out.

"Chart music isn't a problem," Felix says proudly. "Old and classical stuff I might struggle with."

"That's perfect," Ivy says, "because I'm quite good with classical stuff. My dad has Classic FM on all the time in our house."

"Great!" Felix nods. "What about politics?"

"I'll take charge on politics," Holly jumps in. "That's what I want to study at university."

"Brilliant. It's all starting to make sense as to why each of us was picked for the team. Clearly, they made sure that we could cover lots of topics between us."

Felix hesitates, turning to look at me. The room falls silent and Jacob shifts in his seat uncomfortably.

"Charmley?" Felix says. "Are you able to contribute ... *anything*?"

"Um..." I gulp. "I ... uh..."

He sighs heavily, rolling his eyes. "Anything. Come on. There must be something you can bring to the table."

I bite my lip, racking my brain. There is one thing I can think of. I'm not sure how well it will go down but saying anything right now is better than this awkward silence.

"I'm ... well, uh ... I'm good at witch history," I mumble, so quietly that no one hears it.

"What?" Felix says, looking confused. "Did you say 'history'?"

"I said—"

"Hang on, I remember now that you did do well on your history homework last term," he says, looking hopeful. "Miss Campbell read some of your essays out to the class."

I stare at him, wide-eyed. He's right. I did do very well at history last term. What he doesn't know is that I was using magic spells the entire time to improve my grades.

"That's great," Holly chimes, nodding encouragingly at me. "No one has said history, yet. Morgan, that can be your area of expertise."

"But—"

"That must have been why they picked you," Felix says, looking irritated that I might prove useful. "Right, Charmley, you take history. And don't let us down."

"S-sure," I squeak, my mouth suddenly very dry as the rest of the team beams at me. "I won't let you down."

CHAPTER

+ Nine +

I still haven't told Mum about the letter.

It has been a whole week and I haven't quite found the right moment. I haven't got very far in working out whether my assumption about my dad being a warlock is true or not. Google isn't exactly very helpful when it comes to these things. Merlin thinks it's time I told Mum so that I can get to the bottom of it.

"You need to tell her," he says on Saturday afternoon, hanging upside down from my bedroom curtain rail in his bat form. "You're in denial."

"I am not in denial," I argue, trying to focus on homework. Somehow, I'm already behind.

"Yes, you are," he insists. "Otherwise, you'd just ask her to tell you the truth. But you're too scared to hear the truth."

"I am not scared."

"Then ask her!"

"How am I supposed to ask such an important question?" I huff, throwing down my pen. "Just drop it in over breakfast? Mum, please can you pass me the orange juice – oh, and by any chance is my dad a warlock named Maverick?" I shake my head. "It's not exactly an easy topic to bring up."

He swoops down and lands on my desk. "Don't you want to know once and for all, though? You've been torturing us all week."

I let out a sigh. "Fine. Maybe I can bring it up this weekend."

"No time like the present," he says, turning into a monkey and running across the floor to open the door.

I shoot him a look and reluctantly push myself up from my chair. I get the letter from my drawer and carefully slide it into my back pocket. I find Mum in her office, typing furiously at her computer. Her familiar Helena is in the form of an eagle, perching on top of a pile of books.

"It doesn't look like it's a good time," I whisper to Merlin, who is a spider on my shoulder. "I'll talk to her late—"

"Morgan?"

Mum swivels round in her chair and smiles at me.

"Oh! Hey, Mum!" I say breezily, pretending as though I'd been passing. "Whassup?"

"*Whassup?*" Merlin whispers, sounding repulsed.

"I feel like we haven't seen each other much this week," Mum comments, gesturing for me to come into the room.

"I know. You've been so busy with work. How's the project?"

"It's all right," she says, scrunching up her eyes and pinching the top of her nose. "Stressful, but we'll get there. The client is very particular when it comes to their vision. How is your quiz team going? All those early morning meetings must be paying off!"

"Sure," I lie, hoping that she never talks to anyone else on the team and discovers we haven't had a single early morning meeting. "It's going great. I'm full of knowledge."

"Well done, you." She grins. "I'm proud of you."

"Right back atcha."

"Jeez," Merlin groans. "Just ask her."

"What's Merlin saying?" Helena says, shooting my shoulder a disapproving look with her beady eagle eye. She has never been Merlin's biggest fan. "I can hear him whispering something to you. I hope he's not being discouraging about the quiz team."

"You would be too, if you'd heard some of Morgan's answers to the practice questions." Merlin sniggers, turning into a pigeon and flying to land on Mum's desk, purposefully trampling all over some important-looking documents. "She guessed that the winged horse in Greek mythology was called 'Wing-Horse'."

"Thank you, Merlin," I say through gritted teeth. "I now know that the answer is, of course, Theseus."

"Pegasus, you dungbrain," he sighs. "Theseus killed the Minotaur."

"OK, well, why do all their names end in 'us'?" I cry. "It's so confusing!"

"I think you're going to do brilliantly," Mum says, giving Merlin a stern look before yanking the documents out from under his scrawny pigeon toes. "And anyway, it's the taking part that matters."

Mum notices an email ping up on her screen, momentarily turning away to read it. Merlin starts signalling at me to bring up the dad thing by jerking his head towards her.

"Uh ... Mum?" I say nervously. "Can I ask you a question?"

"Of course." She turns back to face me. "What do you want to ask?"

"It's about ... warlocks."

She shudders. "What about them?"

"Um. Are they . . . are they all bad?"

"Yes," she says, without hesitation.

"All of them? All the time?"

"Yes." She frowns at me. "Why are you asking?"

"No reason," I squeak. "I was curious. I thought that maybe there were some exceptions to that rule. Like how you can get some bad witches. Maybe you can also get some good warlocks?"

"Warlocks are all bad. There are no exceptions," she says gravely.

I bite my lip, avoiding eye contact with Merlin. "Have you always thought that?"

"What do you mean exactly?"

It's at times like this that I realize just how businesslike my mum can be. She is very direct and intense, always precise, no rambling. It can be very disconcerting.

"I mean, have you always disliked warlocks?"

"Yes, of course. Witches and warlocks have been at odds with one another for centuries, it's not a recent stance."

"But warlocks help us, don't they?" I point out. "They give us memory-wiping potion and we help them when they get stuck with a magical issue. Doesn't that make us more like . . . two groups who may not get on but at least *understand* one another?"

Mum blinks at me. Helena looks accusingly at Merlin.

"Hey, don't look at me," he says, ruffling his feathers. "I hate warlocks and have trained her to be of the same belief."

"You haven't trained me in anything," I tell him crossly.

"Morgan," Mum begins with a serious expression, "we are obliged to help warlocks and they are obliged to help us in order to protect the one and only thing we have in common: magic. History has taught us that it is best for our magic ability to be a secret. Unfortunately, that means we have to occasionally step in to help each other. But aside from that, witches will never look on warlocks as anything but a terrible inconvenience." She pauses. "Is this about the necklace?"

"The necklace?" I gulp, my hand instinctively shooting upwards to my pendant, but luckily it's hidden beneath my jumper. "What about the necklace?"

"Well, you know that it was given to your great grandmother by a warlock," she explains, watching me closely. Something about the way she's looking at me makes a shiver go down my spine. Like she's reading my mind. "I wondered if that's where all these questions about warlocks have come from?"

"Oh. Yeah. That makes sense."

"It can be of no surprise that warlocks may fall in love with a witch. We are the perfect specimen and vastly superior. But the idea of reciprocating those feelings!" She winces. "The idea of liking a warlock, even hypothetically, is simply impossible. And yes, I have always felt this way towards warlocks, and always will. Like every witch that has ever walked this earth. Warlocks and witches cannot be friends."

"Right." I nod, swallowing the lump in my throat. "Thanks. That answers my question."

"Was there something else you wanted to ask?" she says, her eyebrows knitted together. "You seem ... confused."

"Nope. Nope, I'm not confused," I say as brightly as possible.

"I should have been crystal clear about all this when I gave you the necklace last year. I thought you knew how it was when it comes to warlocks."

"I do know. I just ... I was thinking about the necklace the other day and wondered if my great grandmother had liked that warlock, because she kept the necklace. It didn't make sense to me, but I wanted to check."

"I see."

"Actually, Mum, there was something else I wanted

to ask. Do you mind if I go to a friend's house this afternoon? They ... um ... they're helping me with the quiz. I was worried to ask you as I know we haven't spent much time together."

"Of course you can," she says, visibly relaxing. "I have a lot of work to do anyway. Just make sure you're home for dinner."

"Great."

"Morgan?" she says suddenly, stopping me as I turn to go. "Are you sure there wasn't something else?"

"I'm sure," I reply, shooting her a big, innocent smile as Merlin flies across the room to land on top of my head. "See you in a bit."

I escape from her study as quickly as possible, running down the stairs, grabbing my coat and heading out the door. I send a quick text on my phone and, thankfully, get a speedy reply.

"What was all that about?" Merlin seethes, in his spider form, hidden now that we're out in public.

"She's lying to me. Everything she just said was a lie."

"How do you know?"

"I can tell." I shove my hands into my pockets angrily. "She doesn't quite believe it herself, but she's trained herself to, if that makes sense. I think she fell in love with a warlock, and I think my great grandmother did, too."

"So, where are we going?" Merlin asks, confused.

"We are going to track down my dad and get the truth. But I'm going to need someone's help first," I explain, turning the corner. "We're going to meet them."

"Who?"

"Think about it, Merlin. The best way to find a warlock is through a warlock," I say determinedly. "And we only know one of those."

Owen reads the letter several times before he looks up. We've met on the bench in the park, but it's only us this time. I got an earful from Merlin on the way here, complaining about my idea as soon as I told him we were going to meet Owen to get his help, but now that we're here, I know I've made the right decision. Even just someone else knowing about all this has made me feel better. It's been difficult to handle on my own.

"Morgan. . ." Owen begins gently, his voice trailing off.

"I'm OK," I reply, guessing what his question was going to be. "It was a bit of a shock, but I'm OK now. I want to find out the truth."

"Has your mum ever told you anything about your dad?"

I shake my head. "No. Nothing. I thought he was a spy."

"A spy," he repeats. "As in . . . a James-Bond-type spy?"

"Yeah." I shrug. "All this time, I thought that's why he was forced to leave and why he wasn't allowed to get in touch with me. But it turns out, he wasn't forced to do anything. He chose to stay away because . . . he's a magical enemy."

Owen looks down at the letter again. "Do you think that he's—"

"A warlock?" I say as he purses his lips. "Yeah, I do. Do you?"

He nods. "I can't think what else he could mean."

"I want to find him." I fiddle with my necklace nervously. "I know that sounds strange, but I—"

"It doesn't sound strange," he jumps in, his forehead furrowed. "It isn't strange that you want to find your dad."

"Can you help me?" I ask hopefully.

Owen raises his eyebrows. "Me?"

"I was hoping you might have better links to the warlock community," I explain. "I know just his first name, which is not much to go on. I know it's asking a lot, but I think you might be able to help. And I don't want my mum to know about it. Not yet."

"OK. I'll see what I can do."

"Really?" I'm taken aback at how easy it was to rope

him into this plan. "Are you sure? Do you think we might be able to find him?"

"We can try." He shrugs, offering me a smile. "No harm in trying."

"Thanks so much," I gush, fighting the urge to give him a hug. "I thought you'd tell me it was a terrible idea and that I was being stupid. I'd planned on giving myself at least a week to persuade you."

"Most of your ideas are terrible, to be honest." He laughs. "But if it was the other way round, I know that you'd help me, right?"

I nod, thoughtfully. "Right."

"As long as you're sure you want to find him," he warns, locking my eyes with his. "And you're prepared for the possibility that he might not want to be found."

"I'm sure," I say firmly. "And if he doesn't want to be found by me, then that's OK. You can't miss what you never had. But by the sound of this letter, he wanted me to know his story. This is his chance to tell me how it goes."

"All right, then," Owen says. "The Maverick Mission is officially go."

I smile gratefully, before I notice him squinting his eyes at me.

"What?" I ask.

"Your necklace. . ." He points at the pendant, which is now on show due to my fiddling with it throughout our conversation. "I thought it was blue. But it's changed colour. It's almost black."

I look down to see that it is darker than it was this morning.

"Yeah, it's strange. I don't know why it's different all of a sudden. I don't think it means anything, though."

"Your mum gave it to you, didn't she? So, it's probably magical?" Owen asks, excited at the prospect of a magical mystery. "Is there a story behind it? Maybe we can work out from that why it changes colour."

"Wish it was that interesting," I say quickly, tucking the necklace back under my jumper. "But there's no story. I think she just found it at a cheap market stall somewhere."

Owen looks mildly disappointed not to solve the puzzle, but moves the conversation on.

Meanwhile, Merlin sits quietly next to us as a black cat, his bright yellow eyes on me the whole time, his tail flicking back and forth.

CHAPTER

✦ Ten ✦

It's the day of the first round of the quiz and I am SO not prepared.

In my defence, I've had a lot going on recently and my head has not been in the game. I've tried to sit down and study as much as possible, but between homework and getting lost in thoughts about the possibility of finding my dad, it's been very hard to focus on much else.

Broomstick-flying lessons are usually the best way to clear my head, but, having only taken it up at the end of last year, I'm still not allowed to go out flying without Mum or Dora, and they've been so busy recently, we haven't been out in weeks. I miss it.

"Morgan, I hope you're on better form than yesterday," Felix growls at me on the bus on the way to Woodvale

School, where the first round is being hosted. "You were rubbish in the practice round."

I ignore him, turning to look out the window as we drive through the flat Essex countryside. Holly, sitting next to me, nudges my arm and gives me an encouraging smile. The team is mostly sitting quietly – apart from Felix, who won't shut up – at the front of the coach, while loads of other students coming to support us are taking up the rest of it. Iris, Lucy and Owen are giving up their evening to be part of the audience and are sitting together a few rows behind, chatting and laughing, free of nerves.

My stomach is twisted into knots. I've considered getting out of it by faking illness, but I think that would be worse than taking part and not contributing anything. Felix is right about yesterday. I was terrible. Even when I knew the answer, my brain didn't work fast enough and while I paused, Felix kept yelling, "TIME'S UP, CHARMLEY! The other team have won that question. Again."

I want to hate Owen for putting me in this position. But he is also helping me to track down Maverick, which is really nice.

Warlocks are very tricky creatures.

"We're here!" Mr Hopkins announces, standing up in the front row as the bus parks in front of Woodvale.

"Now, remember, you are representing Riddle House. Be on your best behaviour! And quiz team – " he waggles his finger at us – "show them what you're made of."

"YEAH!" Felix cries, jumping to his feet and raising his fist at the rest of the bus. "LET'S KICK THEIR BUTTS!"

The coach erupts into cheers and whoops. I feel like I may be sick any second.

Once we've filed off the bus, we're greeted by the Woodvale headmistress, Miss Gallagher, and a few of the students, clustering behind her and looking unimpressed with our arrival. Miss Gallagher is petite, with curly brown hair and big dark eyes, and you know from sight she's not the sort of person to take any nonsense. Mr Hopkins seems a bit nervous around her, stumbling over his words and being a lot more smiley than normal.

"Nice to see you again, Mr Hopkins," Miss Gallagher says, giving him a warm handshake. "How are the dance classes going?"

"V-very well, thank you, Irene ... sorry ... Miss Gallagher," Mr Hopkins replies, clearing his throat. "And you?"

"I've not quite mastered the salsa like you have. You'll have to give me some tips!"

Mr Hopkins laughs nervously. "S-sure."

"You're all very welcome to Woodvale," she says, addressing the students gathering on the gravel drive. "If your team would like to follow our team to the Green Room – " she nods to the group behind her – "the rest of you can follow me to the hall."

Mr Hopkins falls into step with her as the rest of our students trail behind. The five members of the Woodvale quiz team, who have been huddled together speaking in low voices, turn to face us. I lock eyes with one of them. Her eyes widen in horror. My jaw drops to the floor.

Oh no.

A couple of years ago, my mum encouraged me to make friends with Sandy Cadabra, the daughter of another witch in our coven. As I was still being home-schooled, Mum was keen for me to have a friend my age and thought it would be a great idea to introduce us. I was forced over to Sandy's house one afternoon and our mums left us to it, thinking we'd get on super well, both being witches of the same age.

We had stood there awkwardly for a bit and then she'd spoken.

"How come you're not at a *real* school?"

"I haven't passed my YWE yet."

"What? I passed when I was five. That was *years* ago. Like, five years."

"That's nice. Hopefully I'll pass soon."

"Wow, you must be *really* bad at spells."

So, obviously, I had clicked my fingers and turned her into a cactus. It was HILARIOUS. And she deserved it. But, of course, the grown-ups didn't see it that way. Sandy's mum got really mad and made us leave while she turned her daughter back to normal. Mum went on for days about how I couldn't go around turning those who were mean to me into a cactus.

I told her that if mean people got turned into a cactus more often, maybe they wouldn't be so mean. That would sure sort out a lot of the world's problems.

I thought it was a very good point but I still got grounded.

Apparently Sandy's mum is still very icy towards mine whenever they gather for meetings, and I haven't seen Sandy since.

Until now.

"*Morgan Charmley*," she says venomously, her eyes narrowing to slits. "What are you doing here?"

"*Sandy Cadabra*," I say, awash with a feeling of dread, as the others watch our cold interaction with interest. "Well, well, well."

I'm not sure why I say "well, well, well". It's not really my vibe, but it seems like an appropriate moment to say something along those lines. They always say it in movies when faced with an adversary. I also think that after saying something like "well, well, well" you're supposed to follow it up with a snide comment, but I can't think of anything.

"You two know each other?" Jacob asks eventually, raising his eyebrows.

"Yeah." Sandy nods slowly, her arms folded as she looks me up and down. "We do."

"We'll leave you to your little reunion, then," one of the Woodvale students says, before turning to the rest of my team. "You want to come with us to the Green Room?"

Sandy and I hang back until the others are out of earshot. When they're safely in the building, Sandy's familiar appears in the form of a scorpion on her shoulder, pointing its sting at me threateningly. Merlin turns into a viper, wrapped around my neck, baring fangs at Sandy.

"Merlin, maybe tone it down," I warn, glancing towards the school building. "A snake might be a little out there if anyone's looking from a window."

"Hello, Casper," he hisses at Sandy's familiar, completely ignoring me and staying put as the snake. "We meet again, old nemesis."

"Oh, Merlin," Casper says, lifting his sting, "still so

very bitter. It must be very tough to be the familiar of a failed witch."

"You couldn't begin to comprehend the extent of Morgan's powers," Merlin replies. "Speaking of bitter, sounds like someone's still a bit . . . *prickly.*"

"A cactus spell is so *weak,*" Casper spits, a nerve struck. "Unlike your witch, Sandy has some class. She doesn't feel the need to turn people into objects simply because she can. If she did, your witch wouldn't stand a chance."

"Guess we'll see about that."

"Guess we will."

They glare at each other. Sandy gestures towards the school building.

"Shall we?" she says.

"We shall," I reply.

We walk next to one another, the gravel crunching beneath our feet. Casper transforms into a grasshopper, tucking himself under Sandy's collar, while Merlin changes into a mosquito, hidden on my shoulder. Sandy doesn't say another word to me until we reach a classroom that has a piece of paper stuck to the door reading, *Green Room for Quiz Teams.*

"This should be fun," she says, stopping before we go in to join our teams. "I'm looking forward to beating you in front of a crowd."

"Dream on, Sandy," I reply, a lot more confidently than I feel. "I'm *awesome* at quizzes."

It's not my finest comeback, if I'm honest. For one thing, it's a massive lie and she's going to find that out very soon when the quiz begins, and for another, it's not exactly that threatening. But I lift my chin and march past her into the Green Room as though I've just delivered a devastating blow.

"Morgan," Ivy says, when I come over to join them in one corner of the classroom. "What was that about? How do you know that girl?"

"It's a long story," I say, brushing it off. "But she is the *worst*. We can't let them win."

"Exactly." Felix nods, agreeing with me for the first time ever. "I hate Woodvale."

We glance over towards Sandy and her team, huddled in the far corner, whispering and sniggering. I imagine she's making up some horrible stories about me, probably tweaking the truth, telling them how many exams I've failed.

There's a knock on the door and Owen comes in with Iris, hurrying over to wish us luck before we go on.

"The hall is packed," Owen informs us. "It's quite scary out there."

"Helpful, Owen," Iris says, rolling her eyes before turning to us with a big, positive smile. "Don't worry, you'll smash this. And even if you lose, you've still got three more rounds to win it back."

"Don't speak about losing, Iris," Felix says, appalled. "We're focusing on the WIN."

"Are you OK?" Owen asks me quietly, while the rest of the team chat amongst themselves. "You look nervous. Don't worry, you've got this."

"It's not that," I say, before taking his arm and pulling him to the side. "Don't look over and make it obvious, but there's another witch on their team."

"You're joking."

"Nope. Sandy Cadabra. Her mum is in the same coven as mine. She also hates me."

"That's not good." He looks at me sternly. "No magic though, remember? This has to be a fair competition."

"I wouldn't even consider it," I inform him.

"As if I'm in a room with two witches right now." He shudders. "Gross."

I'm about to launch into our standard argument but stop myself when I notice Iris watching us with a weird look on her face.

"Iris, are you all right?"

"Yeah," she says slowly, looking confused. "It's just . . . something about you two . . . I don't know. Standing together. It reminds me of something."

Owen and I share a look.

"What do you mean?" Owen asks, taking a small step back from me.

"Nothing. It's these weird dreams I'm having. I think you two are in them. I'm not sure, but ... I think you're something to do with the magic." She shakes her head before offering us an apologetic smile. "It sounds so stupid, I know. Sorry, dreams are boring."

"Why would you be dreaming about us?" I say, laughing a little too enthusiastically. "Iris, you are a cuckoo-head sometimes."

Cuckoo-head?

She laughs weakly. "Right."

"Anyway, we should go take our seats, right, Iris?" Owen says hurriedly, heading towards the door. "Good luck, everyone!"

Before he reaches the door, Sandy comes marching over from the other side of the room, her hand outstretched and a sickly sweet smile on her face.

"Hi, I'm Sandy," she says to Owen, ignoring Iris. "So nice of you to come back here and wish your team good luck."

"She's been watching you two talking this whole time," Merlin whispers in my ear. "Whatever she's doing right now, it is some form of sabotage."

"You think she knows he's a warlock?" I whisper back, panicked.

"She can't possibly," he assures me. "If she did, there's no way she'd be so friendly towards him. She'd be cursing him and all his family. No, she's up to something else."

I watch as Owen introduces himself and Iris, before wishing Sandy and the Woodvale team luck, too.

"Thanks, Owen," Sandy replies, tilting her head. "That's really mature of you. There's no reason why there should be any bad blood between the schools. After all, the point of this competition isn't just about rising to a challenge, it's also about making new friends."

"Yeah, I guess," Owen replies, looking a little unnerved. "We're more like ... frenemies."

Sandy bursts out laughing as though he's said the funniest thing in the world. I seethe as Owen looks pleased with himself, not expecting such an enthusiastic reaction.

"See you around," he says, as Iris nudges him towards the door.

"See you, Owen," Sandy replies, wiggling her fingers at him, before flouncing back towards her team.

UGH! Who does she think she is? I know EXACTLY what she's up to.

"That's her plan! I can see right through her," I say on

the sly to Merlin, shooting daggers at Sandy. "She wants to turn all my friends against me!"

"*All* your friends?" he remarks.

"Fine!" I huff. "My one friend!"

"Oi, Charmley, when you've finished talking to yourself," Felix says, irritated, beckoning me back to the group. "You've missed our team strategy."

"It's hardly a strategy," Holly says, looking bored. "All you've said is that we should all play to our strengths, which we already know."

"Don't mock the strategy, Holly," he whispers, staring her down. "*Don't mock the strategy.*"

I think we're all a bit freaked out by Felix, so everyone seems relieved when the Green Room door suddenly swings open and Miss Gallagher appears.

"Right, quiz teams," she announces, clapping her hands together, "are you ready?"

"Oh," Sandy sneers, looking my way with a thin-lipped smile, "we're ready."

"Whatever," I say, meeting her gaze. "We are *readier.*"

"You know what?" Merlin whispers to me, as we begin the walk towards the hall. "We really need to work on your comebacks."

CHAPTER

+ Eleven +

We walk out on to the stage to thunderous applause. I'm so shocked by how big the audience is that I stop in my tracks after a few steps and Ivy has to prod me in the back to get me moving again. I hate this. I hate public speaking. I can barely make it through a presentation in front of my class, let alone answer questions fired at me in front of an entire auditorium.

Forget about Owen being nice to me about the dad thing.

I *really* hate him right now.

There are two tables set up either side of the stage, a Quiz Master desk between them, and behind that, a large scoreboard with an eager Woodvale student standing next to it, ready to tally the points. The auditorium feels bigger than the one at our school and it's a full house, every seat occupied by the audience which seems to stretch on for ever. I squint into the spotlights that come on full beam as we make our way to our seats. I'm already feeling sweaty and hot from the nerves, and the intense lighting isn't ideal.

"Eugh," Merlin grumbles, in his spider form. "I hope you put on deodorant before you left the house."

"Not helping," I say through gritted teeth, stumbling slightly as I pull a chair out and take my place between Jacob and Holly.

The auditorium falls silent as Miss Gallagher walks on to the stage, the clacking of her sensible court-shoe heels echoing off the walls. I take the opportunity to peer out to the audience, a blur of students, teachers and parents of members of the teams. I told Mum she didn't need to worry about coming as it was only the first round and I knew she had to work late, but she insisted Dora come to support me in her place. I spot her fairly quickly – she's sitting in the third row wearing a canary-yellow dress with little ducks stitched all over it. She catches my eye and gives me a thumbs-up.

Miss Gallagher stops centre stage, smiling at the sea of faces looking up at her.

"Welcome to this year's SCHOOL CHALLENGE!"

The audience cheers and claps until she raises her arms in a bid for silence.

"Woodvale School is very honoured to be taking part in such a fun competition with our good friends at Riddle House – " there is a mix of boos and cheers – "and we are delighted to host the first round. We welcome our guests and look forward to an evening of great fun and fascinating facts. The competition consists of four rounds overall, and the team with the most points at the end of the last round will win. The questions today will cover a host of topics, each one designed to challenge our brilliant quiz teams. The structure is simple – I will ask a question and the first student to press their bell and answer correctly receives the point. So, without further ado, let's begin!"

She turns on her heel and marches to the Quiz Master station, receiving rapturous applause for her introduction, while we all shift nervously in our seats.

"Remember," Felix says down the table, reaching forwards to cover his bell with his hands, "play to your strengths."

My mouth is so dry, I reach for the glass of water placed out in front of me a little too eagerly, spilling it as I bring it towards me, the cold water sploshing down the sides and dribbling into my lap. Placing the glass back down, hands shaking, I notice Sandy watching me with a smug smile. I tug at my collar, almost knocking Merlin from his perch on my shoulder. Isn't anyone else noticing how hot it is in here?

"All right, the first topic we're starting with is general knowledge," Miss Gallagher announces, lifting up her quiz cards. "Riddle House, are you ready? Woodvale, are you ready?"

Both teams nod.

"Here we go, then." She clears her throat. "Question One: which swimming stroke is named after an insect?"

Sandy slams her hand down on her bell and its ring echoes around the silent hall.

"Butterfly!" she yells out.

"That is correct!" Miss Gallagher trills and the audience cheers, while the scoreboard is changed to show one point to Woodvale.

Felix pounds his fist on the table, already furious.

"Question Two: how many sides does an octagon have?"

Ivy has pressed her bell before Miss Gallagher's finished the question.

"Eight!"

"That is correct! One point to Riddle House!"

Felix fist bumps Ivy and we all go back to focusing on our bells for the next question.

After three topics – general knowledge followed by sport, and film and music – we are lagging behind and I am yet to contribute an answer. Sandy has, by now, clearly cottoned on to the fact that, contrary to what I claimed, I am in fact NOT awesome at quizzes, and every time she gets an answer right, which is very often, she shoots me this infuriating smile, revelling in her success.

Felix is getting more and more passionate, jumping to his feet and crying out things like "GET IN!" any time we get an answer right, and then slapping his hand on the table and yelling angrily, "OH COME ON, REF!" if Woodvale gets a point. Miss Gallagher has already issued him a warning for when he got a question right about Aston Villa and then climbed on to his chair and did a victory dance, to the crowd's delight.

Miss Gallagher announces it's the history round and, as the rest of the team nods knowingly to me, I desperately wish I could slide under the table and hide there until it's over.

"You could use magic. . ." Merlin whispers.

I shake my head.

As Miss Gallagher prepares her question cards, I wipe the sweat from my forehead, butterflies flitting about in my stomach like crazy. I'm so nervous and worried, I feel like I might faint at any second, but then a lone voice pipes up from the audience.

"COME ON, CHARMLEY! YOU'VE GOT THIS!"

It's Owen. I blink out at the audience, attempting to see him, but I'm not sure which direction his voice came from. His yell encourages everyone else in the crowd and suddenly the hall is filled with cheers for individual team members and the two schools.

I eventually make out Owen sitting at the end of a row on the right-hand side facing the stage. He catches my eye and mimics taking a dramatic breath in and out. I sit up a little higher and take a deep breath, realizing that I've been so nervous, I've almost forgotten to breathe all together.

I've got this.

Maybe.

Do I?

Maybe not.

Oh, shut up, brain!

Miss Gallagher asks for quiet from the audience and, when the hall has fallen silent and our hands are hovering over the bells, she launches into the history round.

The first question is about Queen Victoria, and Sandy is straight in there before my brain can process what's happened, shouting out her answer and receiving a point. While Woodvale celebrates, she catches my eye and mouths, "*loser*".

"Forget the audience and forget Sandy," Merlin instructs. "Just focus on the question. You are NOT going to let Sandy Cadabra get away with calling you a loser. Got it?"

"Got it," I say out loud, receiving a strange look from Holly.

"Question Two," Miss Gallagher says. "When William the Conqueror died in 1087, who succeeded him as King of England?"

Hang on. I know this.

I ACTUALLY KNOW THIS.

I slam my bell with all my might, nearly sending it flying off the table. All eyes turn to me.

"William II," I say nervously, hoping I've remembered it right.

"That is . . . correct!" Miss Gallagher declares.

My heart soars as Riddle House fans cheer in support, while Holly pats me on the back and even Felix brings himself to cry, "YES!" and smile at me. I can't believe I got an answer! I remember about William II from my essays about William the Conqueror last term. I had to read some of them to the class, despite the fact that it was magic and not me who wrote them.

Some of it must have gone into my brain without me realizing.

Getting the answer to that question is the confidence boost I need. It feels really good to get something right. No wonder Sandy has looked so smug this whole time. This feels GREAT.

Woodvale get the next two points, but then a miracle happens.

"In the 1600s, when hysteria gripped the country, a man named Matthew Hopkins decided to become a witch hunter—"

Sandy and I share a startled look. *What are the chances?*

"—imprisoning many women accused of being witches—"

Sandy purses her lips. We may dislike each other, but that's nothing in comparison to how we both feel about Matthew Hopkins, the man who attempted to wipe out witches. Not that he came close. Witches of the time were, of course, completely immune to his punishments and had to go along with the spectacle to keep our secret safe, but his rantings and ravings were extremely insulting.

"—but what was the title he appointed himself?"

Sandy's hand jerks towards her bell, but I get there a millisecond faster.

"The Witchfinder General," I announce confidently.

"Correct!"

"WOOOOOOOOO!" Felix jumps to his feet, cheering along with everyone, before leaning over to give me a high-five.

Sandy looks furious and Merlin can't resist turning into a fly and doing a victory lap around my head to make sure that Casper can see him.

It's a brilliant moment, but our celebrating doesn't last long.

By the end of the quiz, Woodvale are a few points ahead of us. Miss Gallagher gets to her feet and announces the final result, keen to emphasize that both teams did very well. The auditorium reacts to the points – Woodvale cheering at the top of their lungs, Riddle House reluctantly applauding – and the teams are encouraged to get up and shake hands. Merlin groans as Sandy swans across the stage, a triumphant grin plastered across her face as she makes a beeline for me.

"Just as I thought," she says quietly so no one can hear over the applause, "you're about as good at quizzes as you are at spells. And to be clear, I mean that you're absolutely rubbish at both. You're a joke, Morgan Charmley."

In the form of a wasp, Casper cackles, hovering by her hand as she holds it out to me.

Biting my tongue, I shake her hand, with Merlin sitting on my wrist in the form of a spider. The familiars glare at each other in warning.

"See you in the next round." She smiles, dropping my hand and waltzing off the stage towards a group of classmates waiting to congratulate her.

"I can't stand this," Merlin says, once he's scuttled up my arm to my shoulder. "I can't stand this one bit."

"It's not over yet. There are still three rounds to go," I say, lifting my chin and narrowing my eyes at Sandy's back as she walks away. "I won't let her win."

CHAPTER

+ Twelve +

"There you are."

Owen appears at my side as I shove my books back into my locker after school finishes for the day.

"I was looking for you after class," he continues, waiting for me.

"Sorry," I tell him, slamming my locker shut and rolling my eyes. "I was trying to get out of here as fast as possible before Felix could corner me, but he tracked me down and then yelled at me for a bit."

Since the first round of the quiz last week, Felix has gone from being a little bit mad about School Challenge to being absolutely bonkers about it. That very evening, once we'd all gone home, he'd messaged us with a detailed schedule of quiz meetings for the next couple of weeks, telling us that any extra-curricular activities we had on were officially not a priority and all our energy needed to go into practising for the quiz.

It didn't go down that well with Holly, Ivy and Jacob, who all have a lot of music and sport lessons, and also want some free time to stay on top of homework and hang out with friends.

"We did really well, Felix," Ivy had yawned when he'd called us in for an early morning meeting before class started. "I think we should just keep doing what we were doing – study when we can, stick to our strengths and do some practice rounds."

"Yeah, Woodvale are probably going to get complacent now," Jacob had chipped in. "We'll easily win next time."

"Was I the only one there at the last round?" Felix had huffed. "We LOST. I don't lose, OK? I win."

"You lost in the school talent show last term," Holly had pointed out, winking at me. "Morgan's team won."

I'd smiled at her. I couldn't work out why Holly was being nice to me when I was so unpopular, but then I found out that she was on the dance team with Iris and I wondered whether Iris had said nice things about me to her. It's the only explanation I could come up with.

"Charmley had nothing to do with her team winning that talent show," Felix had snapped. "If anything, she almost cost them the win. Well, I'm not going to let that happen this time."

He didn't seem to care that I'd got some of the questions right in the first round, all he cared about was that I got ALL of the questions right next time. He'd analysed our performance and the history round had been our weakest point score – "surprise, surprise," he'd added snidely after announcing this – so if I could improve, then we might have a chance of beating Woodvale next time.

It's a lot of pressure. Every time I see Felix, he yells a question at me and waits for me to answer. When I get it wrong or hesitate, he says, "WOODVALE WIN. Brilliant, thanks, Charmley."

Sometimes I can't even see him, I'll just hear his voice suddenly shout to me in the corridor and I have to answer with no idea where he is.

It's very unnerving.

"I don't think I've ever seen Felix work so hard at anything," Owen points out, leaning on the locker next to mine. "Who knew he could be so motivated?"

"I know, it's weird. I'm used to him being mean and distracted. Now, he's mean and focused. He must *really* want to look good on TV."

"It's fun, though, right?"

"Are you trying to persuade me that you did me a favour by signing me up for this? It's never going to work, Owen, I'm still annoyed. You're lucky I haven't set a swarm of bats on you." I hold up a wodge of paper and wave it in his face. "Felix has given me these history printouts to read, on top of all my homework. Fun! I'll see you tomorrow."

"Wait, you're not coming to Iris's dance thing?"

"What dance thing?"

"She's got a competition on tonight, remember?" he explains. "It's in the sports hall. You were there when she mentioned it the other day. She's captain of the dance team; it's a big deal for her."

We'd been waiting for Miss Campbell to arrive one morning this week and Iris had invited the whole class. I'd completely forgotten about it.

"Is that tonight?" I hesitate, looking down at the history notes. Felix can't get angry about me skipping study to support Iris. He'll probably be in the audience cheering her on, too. It's the perfect excuse. "Sounds great. I'll come."

Aside from Owen, Iris is the only person in our year that notices me and I owe it to her to make an effort considering it's my fault that she's been having all these creepy magical dreams.

"Cool, it starts in half an hour. Which is perfect, because I need to talk to you first." Owen glances around the corridor to check no one is listening and then lowers his voice. "It's about Maverick. Let's find an empty classroom and I'll fill you in."

I follow him through the maze of corridors until we find a classroom in a deserted area. Safely inside, Merlin transforms into a hawk and has a swoop around the room to stretch his wings and show off. Owen shuts the door behind us and reaches into his pocket, pulling out a scrap of paper.

"Here," he begins, holding it out for me, "it's his address."

I stare at him. Merlin immediately lands on my shoulder and transforms into a small monkey, peering at the piece of paper with great interest.

"W-what?"

"I'm almost certain it's him," Owen says quietly but firmly, his forehead furrowed in concern. "He left a clue in the letter about having some links to Bath. At first I tried to search for warlocks named Maverick living there at the moment, but didn't get anywhere. Then I noticed he used the word 'return' in his letter when he was talking about Bath. He wasn't planning on living there, he was *returning* there until he went somewhere else. I figured maybe he grew up there; maybe his parents lived there. It didn't take me long to find out that in Bath there were two warlocks married to each other. Their surname was Moonshine. They'd had a son named Maverick."

Merlin and I share a look before I reach out and take the piece of paper from Owen.

"Once I had his full name, it wasn't difficult at all to find him," Owen explains, shoving his hands in his pockets. "Maverick Moonshine lives in south London."

He hesitates.

"What?" I ask, trying to read his expression. "What are you not saying?"

"Maverick Moonshine is . . . well, he's quite a famous warlock, Morgan. As in, he's a very powerful warlock. Supposedly, one of the best we've ever known. He has a knack for creating new potions. Anyway, that's the address I found for fanmail."

"So, that's that, then," I manage to say, a lump forming in my throat. "This confirms it. My dad is a warlock. A famous warlock."

"It might be a coincidence," Owen offers. "Maybe this is a random warlock who has the same first name as your dad and also has links to Bath. It's not that crazy an idea. We may have got this wrong and your dad isn't a warlock at all. He might be a normal person. I didn't check out all the Mavericks who grew up in Bath. Just the warlocks."

"Sure, except how many normal people do you know who write goodbye letters on parchment and refer to themselves as a 'magical enemy'?"

Owen looks down at his feet. He doesn't say anything.

I read the address on the piece of paper.

"I don't want to show up at his door," I say, biting my lip.

"It might be easier to write to him. I tried to find an email address but I think Maverick isn't really a tech kind of person. From what I've read about him, he sounds quite eccentric and old-school."

I fold the piece of paper back up and put it in my pocket.

"I'll write to him when I get home tonight." I hesitate. "What do you think I should say?"

"What do you want to say?"

"I'm not sure." I sigh, leaning back on a desk. "I can't believe this is happening. I never thought I needed my dad. But ever since I found that letter, I want to know everything about him. That's stupid, right?"

"No, Morgan, that's not stupid. It's normal to want to know who you are."

I bring my eyes up to meet his, before quietly asking,

"Have you ever heard of a witch who had a warlock as a dad?"

Owen shakes his head slowly. "No. I haven't."

"Maybe that's why I failed my YWE so many times," I reason, starting to get a headache from all this serious talk. "My magic is all messed up."

"I vote you don't write to this Maverick person," Merlin chips in, jumping down on to the desk and changing into a black cat. "It's bound to get complicated and that sounds boring. Why don't we forget the whole thing? Pretend it never happened and stick to our ambitions of you being the most powerful and evil witch that ever walked the earth!"

I roll my eyes.

"You really won the jackpot when it came to spirit guides, didn't you?" Owen states, smiling at me. Merlin glares at him, before baring his cat claws and getting into a pounce position.

"Don't even think about it," I warn Merlin, shooting him a stern look. "You say much worse to him usually."

"Yeah, well, he deserves it, being a smelly warlock," Merlin grumbles.

"I think it's time we went to the dance competition," Owen says, laughing off Merlin's comment. "You can think about all this later."

"Sure. And, Owen," I say, as we get ready to leave the classroom, "thanks so much for all this. For finding him. I owe you one."

"You know what you can do in return?" he replies, grinning at me as he holds open the door. "Never, ever tell anyone that I willingly helped a witch."

It takes me a few days to finish drafting the letter to Maverick. In the end, I keep it short and simple. I tell him who I am, say I found a letter that I think he wrote to my mother years ago, and ask him to please write back. I include my address, but not my phone number. I don't want him to call me out of the blue when I'm at school or something.

I carry the letter around with me for two weeks.

Then, one Saturday morning, I happen to pass a postbox. Without noticing, I realize I've stopped and I'm standing in the middle of the pavement, staring at it.

"It's time," Merlin says simply. "Otherwise, I suppose, we'll always wonder."

I unzip my bag, pull the crumpled letter out and, taking a deep breath, I post it.

And now, I wait.

CHAPTER

✦ Thirteen ✦

I feel like I've been hit by a bus.

Seriously, I've never been this tired in my life. It's all my own fault, too, which is annoying because I can't blame anyone else for feeling this rubbish. I don't know how I let this happen, but one minute the second round of the quiz was ages away and I didn't need to worry about it quite yet, and the next minute, it's today. I was up all night cramming as much information as possible into my brain, any key historical moments that might come up this afternoon. Merlin is grumpier than ever because I kept him up, too, by having the light on and every now and then practising shouting out the answers. By breakfast, he's snapped at me several times. I kept meaning to go through the practice questions from Felix in the evenings and at the weekends, but things kept getting in the way.

Firstly, Mum's work let up a bit, so she suggested some broomstick-flying lessons on weekday evenings and I couldn't really say no. I haven't been flying in ages and I've missed it. There's nothing like soaring through the crisp night air, hidden under the cloak of darkness, flying that little bit faster every time as I get to grips with all the broomstick skill. And Mum has also noticed that I've been avoiding her recently. She doesn't think it's anything *she's* done – she's convinced that something is going on at school that I don't want to talk to her about.

"You can always come to me if you're worried about anything," she keeps saying, whenever she pokes her head round my bedroom door. "If there's anything you want to talk about, even embarrassing things."

"OK, thanks, Mum," I continue to reply, without bothering to look up. "I'm fine, though."

What I really want to say is something along the lines of: "To be honest, Mum, I'm a little bit angry with you right now because YOU HAVE LIED TO ME MY ENTIRE LIFE."

So, I felt that if I turned down flying lessons, she would be even more worried which would cause *more* probing, and I don't want to put up with that right now.

I want her to leave me alone until I hear back from this Maverick person. Then I'll work out where to go from there. If I hear back from him, that is. Still, I'd like to give him a bit more time. It's only been a few days since I sent the letter.

It has been nice sneaking out to the nearby woodland with Mum and Dora late at night, finding our clearing that we always start at, and climbing on to my broomstick. The moment I click my fingers and then lift off from the ground, I forget everything else. I forget to be mad at Mum, even. She always flies along beside me, grinning and shouting instructions like, "OK, try turning a sharp left in a few metres! Remember to stay focused if you want a lovely, smooth flight."

I'm getting quite good at flying now and Mum says she's seen a fresh wave of determination in me the past week.

"I wonder why that could be," Merlin had muttered after she'd said that.

"What do you mean?"

"Oh please," he'd sighed, watching me with beady red eyes as he sat in his albino rat form. "It's so obvious. You're trying to prove that you're a witch. A proper witch flies a broomstick. But I'm afraid that proves nothing."

I'd shaken my head at him and pretended to

concentrate on something else, but we both knew he was right.

As well as broomstick-flying lessons taking up my time, I've been trying not to fall too far behind with homework, which is a lot more difficult now that I'm not using magic to help me along. I even made a very pretty colour-coded schedule, allotting evening hours to specific homework assignments. But no amount of coloured pens can force me to do something that is mind-numbingly boring. I have an extraordinary talent for staring at my textbooks but not actually doing any work, realizing later that I've wasted half an hour doodling bats and toads and stars next to the paragraph I'm supposed to be reading.

And I've also been busy cheering on Iris with her dance team. She was BRILLIANT in the show we went to the day Owen told me about Maverick, and it was so much fun to be part of the crowd supporting her. She won the contest that night and we all went to this cool milkshake bar afterwards to celebrate. For a while I couldn't work out why I felt so elated sitting next to Owen and the rest of his group, sipping a strawberry milkshake and pretending to be interested in Lucy's lengthy story about the time she saw a celebrity I'd never heard of, but then it hit me that it's because I was doing something that normal teenagers do all the time. Something I was longing for last term. I was hanging out with friends.

When Iris mentioned that the team were taking part in another show earlier this week, I didn't even hesitate to say I'd be there. It was so much fun the last time and she seemed genuine when she invited me.

"I'm really glad that you're coming," she'd said cheerily. "And it looks like you and Felix are becoming better friends because of the quiz, which is great!"

"I'm not sure," I'd told her with a knowing smile. "The other day in P.E., he asked me if I ran like a pigeon on purpose for laughs, or if that was just my natural style. Now, I don't ever want to run again."

"Ignore him, he's just jealous."

I'd almost choked on my own spit at that one. "WHAT? Jealous of me?"

"Yeah, course," she'd insisted, thumping me on the back as I'd coughed and spluttered. "He's territorial of Owen. They used to hang out all the time and, now, Owen prefers to hang out with you mostly. Not that I blame him."

I didn't know what to say to that. I'd never thought about it that way. Is that why Felix hated me so much? Because he was worried I was stealing his best friend?

He has always irrationally disliked me. I'd put that down to him thinking I was a big freak who had pet tarantulas and brought them secretly to school, but maybe that was only part of the reason.

After Iris had made that point, I'd decided to make an extra effort to be nice to Felix. We had all seen a different side to him recently, with this whole quiz thing and how seriously he'd been taking it, so maybe he was just as insecure and anxious as the rest of us.

Maybe Felix and I could be friends.

"Good morning, Felix!" I say as brightly as possible, arriving at our classroom.

I don't feel bright at all. I feel like I might collapse in an exhausted heap at any moment.

"You look terrible," he replies, wrinkling his nose. "Seriously. What happened? Did you fall over and get two black eyes at the same time?"

"Shut up, Felix," Iris says, whacking him over the head. "Like you ever look good in the morning."

"Ouch!" His hands fly to his hair. "Iris, don't knock out any brain cells! I don't know if you remember, but it happens to be the second round . . ."

". . . of the quiz today," Iris, Lucy and Owen all chorus.

"Yes, we know," Kareen sighs, rolling her eyes. "You've

mentioned it, oh I don't know, maybe eight hundred times?"

"And that's just today," Zoey adds, looking up from doing some last-minute homework due this afternoon. "It's just a quiz, Felix."

"It's more than that," Felix says, sticking his chin out proudly. "It's going to be the making of my career. I'll be signed up for a reality show by the end of the last round and leaving you suckers behind as I make my way into a world of fame and fortune."

"Sure, very realistic," Iris comments.

Felix shoots me a sharp look as he notices me try and fail to stifle a yawn.

"I hope you're on good form today, Charmley," he spits. "You don't exactly look raring to go."

"I'm fine," I say, using all the energy I have left to stop my eyelids from drooping. "I was up late studying, that's all. I'm very prepared for today."

"True dedication." Iris grins.

Felix snorts, shaking his head in disgust. "Last-minute panic more like. You better be ready. The questions for this round are supposed to be harder and we need to beat Woodvale, otherwise we might as well give up and not bother with the next two rounds. I don't want you to make me look bad."

"Don't you worry," I say, giving him a weak thumbs-up. "I could beat Woodvale in my sleep."

"Which, at this rate, is a genuine possibility," Merlin whispers into my ear, in the form of a gnat. "I bet that you don't even make it to lunch."

Thanks to my good friend, Coffee, Merlin loses his bet and I make it all the way to the end of the day.

It's definitely not a *good* day, though. I barely concentrate on a word in any of the lessons because I keep eyeing up the floor and wondering how comfortable it would be to take a quick nap. At one point, Joe has to nudge me sharply in the ribs when Miss Campbell asks me a question and I don't answer because I'm too busy staring at the carpet with my eyes glazed over.

"Sorry, what did you ask me?" I say, snapping myself out of the daze, wishing I could curl up under the desk. "Something about . . . breakfast?"

"Not quite," Miss Campbell says, pointedly clearing her throat as the class titters at my answer. "I was talking about Francis Bacon."

Felix groans loudly from the other side of the classroom, burying his head in his hands and saying repeatedly, "We're doomed!" until Miss Campbell tells him to be quiet.

By the time the quiz team are sent to gather at the school gates to welcome Woodvale, I'm ready to go home.

"Not very clever to do all this on no sleep," Merlin comments unhelpfully, as I lean on the gates for support. "You've had a lot of late nights from flying lessons, too."

"As my familiar, maybe you should have given me a bit more guidance," I say, irritated. "From what I can remember, you were encouraging me *not* to sit around and study."

"Yeah, because it's boring listening to you get answers wrong all the time."

The Woodvale coach draws up to the school and the rest of the team immediately straighten up and put their game faces on. I would straighten up and put on an intense expression if I had the energy. But I don't.

"Miss Gallagher, welcome!" Mr Hopkins announces, stepping forward to shake her hand as she approaches us, her students following behind.

I've noticed that Mr Hopkins has combed his hair for the occasion and, while waiting with us, straightened his tie at least four times.

"We're excited to be here," Miss Gallagher declares, as he gestures for her to follow him towards the school.

Sandy looks even more smug and haughty than before, putting her hands on her hips as she stops by the gates. Her eyes scan the school building and she wrinkles her nose, unimpressed.

"So, this is Riddle House," she says, flicking her hair behind her shoulders. "The school for losers."

Felix clenches his fists as her team members laugh and give each other high-fives.

"The only losers today will be you," he says, defiantly, as we all nod in agreement.

"We'll see." She glances at me and sneers. "You look as tired as your school, Morgan."

"Yeah, well, you look as stupid as . . . a stupid . . . bug," I retort.

While my team all look embarrassed on my behalf, Sandy simply ignores me, striding towards the main building with her entourage before any of us can offer to take them to our Green Room.

"Come on," Felix hisses to us, hurrying to catch up with them as they reach the steps.

"What am I going to do, Merlin?" I ask, hanging back. "I've messed this up big time."

"I'm not going to argue with you," he replies. "You really have messed this up. You're definitely not ready and you are absolutely going to lose."

"*MERLIN!* What shall I do?"

"You know what to do," he says, sounding irritated as

he buzzes around my head in his wasp form. "If you want to win, you're going to need some *help*."

"Duh! That's what I'm asking you for!"

"You really are slow today. I'm talking about MAGIC."

I stop on the steps as everyone disappears through the doors.

"What?"

Merlin lands on my shoulder and turns into a spider.

"Magic," he repeats. "That's the only way you're going to win this thing."

I shake my head. "I can't do that. Remember what happened last term? And it's cheating."

"How do you know Sandy hasn't been using magic? She could have been cheating all along."

"But . . . I can't. Maybe we still have a chance," I say, desperately trying to convince myself. "I may not be on top form today, but I'll have another coffee. I'm sure loads of the facts I read last night went into my brain. And the rest of my team are brilliant, so it doesn't matter if I drop the ball a bit."

"Last time you did quite well, and your team still lost." He scuttles under my collar. "I'm just saying, if you feel yourself lagging behind, a little bit of magic is always an option."

*

We're losing.

The quiz is in full flow and Woodvale are storming ahead in the points. Even if I'd got some sleep last night, I'd still be no match for Sandy.

"How many energy drinks has that girl had?" Holly remarks, as Sandy once again beats her to an answer, celebrating by punching the air as the hall erupts with applause before sticking her tongue out at me.

I narrow my eyes at her. *Is she really this good?*

What if Merlin is right? What if she is using magic? It would make sense. After the cactus incident, she'd surely never let me humiliate her again. She was bragging in the Green Room before we came on about how she's been studying every night since the first round, but she did look a bit shady when she said it, as though she wasn't being completely honest. Even Holly has picked up on the fact that Sandy seems to be absurdly energetic. She thinks it's Red Bull, but I know better.

And, *technically*, it's not like Woodvale would be at a disadvantage if I used magic. Each team has one witch. It's balanced very fairly. I'm not stopping Sandy from using magic, which she might very well be doing at the moment. So, it wouldn't really be cheating.

I wouldn't have to use magic for ALL the questions, that would be ridiculous. But I could give us a little nudge. Close the gap a bit. Everyone would be bored if there was no competition, right? So, using magic to help wouldn't just be for me and the Riddle House team, it would be for everyone involved.

Now that I think about it, it almost seems quite selfless.

As Sandy's bell jolts me from my thoughts, I watch her celebrate getting another point for Woodvale. I look out at the audience. Iris, in the front row, is biting her lip. Owen has slid down in his seat in dismay. Glancing down the line at my team, I notice that Felix looks like he might burst into tears, his dreams of signing with a TV agent fading. Holly seems to be furious with herself, and Jacob and Ivy both have their eyebrows furrowed in desperate concentration.

My mind is made up. Magic is the only answer. I'm not doing this for me. This is for my team and for the school.

I take a deep breath and close my eyes, thinking about which spell would work best. When I've decided, I lower my hand into my lap and click my fingers determinedly, the sound muffled by the cheering audience as Woodvale score another point.

I open my eyes and glance down at the top of my hand. I can feel it tingling.

I smile to myself. The magic is working.

"Next question," Mr Hopkins announces from the Quiz Master seat, looking deflated by our performance. "Which famous address is located at postcode SW1A 2AA?"

I slam my hands on the bell first. Quick as a flash, words appear on my hand.

"Ten Downing Street!" I call out.

"That is CORRECT!" Mr Hopkins cries, unable to keep the glee from his voice.

The Riddle House side of the audience jump to their feet, clapping and cheering, while the team nods at me, looking a little perked up. The words have already disappeared from my hand, having only stayed etched in my skin for a couple of seconds. It's a very nifty spell, if I do say so myself.

Mr Hopkins waits for the crowd to settle and launches into the next question.

"Which is the longest river in Britain?"

My bell echoes through the hall.

"The Severn!" I yell, after a stealthy glance at my hand.

"ANOTHER POINT FOR RIDDLE HOUSE!"

As Felix leans over to clap me on the back and the others sit up in their seats, a glimpse of hope returning to our team, I smile smugly across the stage at a sour-faced Sandy.

"Well, what do you know?" Merlin sniggers in my ear. "The witch is back."

CHAPTER

+ Fourteen +

We WIN.

When Mr Hopkins declares Riddle House the winner, I am deafened by the audience reaction. Felix is so excited, he jumps on to the TABLE and starts doing the craziest celebratory dance, wiggling his hips and punching the air.

I think I've got away with the whole magic thing, too. I made sure that I didn't overdo it, letting Woodvale get some points here and there, and letting my teammates jump in when they knew the answer. I just made sure we were enough points ahead this time to be drawing with them overall going into the third round.

Sandy looks as though someone has slapped her round the face. She can't believe that she hasn't won. I notice one of her teammates start clapping politely at our win and Sandy rounds on them furiously for showing us any support. I should have known she'd be a sore loser, a tad on the dramatic side.

She really overreacted that time I turned her into a cactus.

My popularity goes up a few points after the win and my mishaps from last term seem to be mostly forgotten. When I walk down the school corridor the next day, I get some encouraging comments from students like, "Good luck for the next round, Morgan!" and "You rock, Charmley!" I feel like I'm in an American high-school movie, but instead of being a loser, I'm one of the jocks or something.

It's pretty cool.

I do feel a *little* bit bad about using magic. It feels like I've tricked everyone into thinking I'm something I'm not, but I promise myself that for the next two rounds I will NOT use magic. I'm going to make sure I'm much better prepared. For one thing, I won't be falling asleep at the quiz table, and for another, I'm going to be very dedicated and put time aside to revise and practise. It was important that we won that round so we at least had a chance at winning overall. I couldn't let my teammates down, not when they've worked so hard.

The only person who is acting a little bit suspicious is, of course, Owen.

WHY does he have to be so righteous? Warlocks are supposed to be horrible human beings: evil, power-grabbing and all for cheating to win. Yet I have to find the ONLY warlock on the planet who makes me feel guilty for using my magic for personal gain. It's so boring.

At first, he wonders aloud how I possibly knew some of those answers and comments on how weird it was that I was so tired and then, suddenly, had more energy than both teams put together. I think about telling Owen the truth, but I decide that his *best* reaction would be to tell me off and lecture me about how I'm breaking rules by using magic at school, and his *worst* reaction would be guilting me into coming clean and telling Mr Hopkins that I cheated so our team could win. Neither of those options is attractive, so I stick to lying.

"I had an espresso before I went on and it must have kicked in halfway through," I tell him breezily, as though I have simply no idea what he's implying. "And I told you that I crammed on general knowledge the night before, right? I think School Challenge must have included some generic questions because, I hate to admit it, but I think I'd read through some of those questions on the practice quizzes."

He looks unconvinced but apparently decides to drop it.

It feels good to be on the team for something the whole school is behind. Our class is buzzing about the win and even the teachers are getting excited about the next two rounds. I bumped into Mr Hopkins in the canteen the day after the quiz and he smiled at me and went, "Ah! One of our star students." ME! A star student! I've never been a star at anything.

It's nice to be a star.

The biggest change is Felix. I notice it a couple of days after the quiz when Owen invites him to join our study group.

The study group is Owen's idea. Our homework this week for Miss Campbell is to each prepare a presentation on a Tudor of our choice and Owen thinks it would be more fun to work on it together. I agree, especially as I'm not very good at motivating myself, so it will be quite handy to be forced to sit down and put it together, plus we can also practise presenting it to an audience. At first, we're not sure where to meet as neither of us wants to go to the other one's house. I can't exactly relax in Owen's house when his warlock mum is around and I guess he feels the same way about my mum, but magnified considering she is the Great Sorceress.

"She's basically the queen of witches," he says with a shudder. "I don't want to go anywhere *near* her."

"Wait, if she's the queen, that makes me the princess, right?" I point out thoughtfully, prompting Owen to roll his eyes. "Does that mean I should be treated like royalty?"

Owen tells me it does not.

Our problems are solved when Mum tells me that she needs to go into the office on Saturday afternoon, because her advertising project has become a nightmare again. Apparently the client has changed their mind and they're back to square one. She's really apologetic about it, but I tell her that I'll be busy anyway with the study group.

"Dora is away this weekend, so you don't need to worry about any witches being around," I inform Owen on Friday morning before registration, keeping my voice down so no one else in the noisy classroom can hear us. "Howard is going to check in on us. He's a normal person, with no clue he's married to a witch, so we're all good."

"Brilliant, thanks." Owen smiles, pleased that we're not going to have to study in the park, which was our original plan.

"What are you guys talking about?" Iris asks, appearing at my side and making me jump.

"We . . . uh . . . a study group!" I say hurriedly. "We're having a study group tomorrow afternoon at my house for the presentation. Would you like to come?"

"At your house? Yes!" She nods enthusiastically. "Sounds good. Thanks!"

"Hey, Felix," Owen yells out across the classroom, before turning to ask me quietly, "All right if I invite him, too? He'll be annoyed if he finds out we left him out."

"Sure," I say with a shrug, even though my heart sinks at the idea.

Felix looks up from a game he's playing on his phone, reluctantly pauses it and makes his way across the classroom to sit on the desk Owen is leaning on.

"What?" he asks.

"We're having a study group tomorrow at Morgan's house. You around?"

"Dad and I are going to a match tomorrow," he says, before looking back down at his phone and starting up his game again. "Sounds fun, though."

My jaw drops to the floor. I can't believe Felix just said that a study group at mine *sounds fun*. As though, if he wasn't busy, he might actually consider joining us. A week ago, he'd have made a snide remark about not wanting to catch freak germs from my house or something, but now he thinks hanging out at my house SOUNDS FUN.

I'm pleased he can't come though; I'm already nervous enough about Owen and Iris coming over. I realize with a growing sense of dread that I've never had friends over to my house before. What are you supposed to do? Do I need to provide snacks? In movies they always provide snacks! I need to buy crisps. And drinks. Lots of different juices and soft drinks. I also have to make sure that the house is tidy and there's no weird magic stuff anywhere. Do I need to create a designated study area? Will everyone need a desk?

ARGH, I've just remembered about the baby photos! I need to hide the baby photos of me that Mum has up EVERYWHERE. What if Iris and Owen see one and then laugh at how big my head was when I was born? They might tell the whole school about my big baby head and then I'll lose all the respect I've just earned from the quiz! I don't want anyone to know about my big baby head! (The doctors said I'd grow into it. My ears remain a little on the large side.)

This study group is a BIG mistake.

"What are you so worried about?" Merlin asks me in his spider form as school finishes for the day and we head out. "You're all sweaty again. What's wrong with your sweat glands?"

"My sweat glands are fine! I'm nervous because I

don't want Owen and Iris to come over tomorrow and then think I'm weird."

"Owen already thinks you're weird because of the witch thing. And Iris thinks you're weird because . . . well . . . you are very weird."

"Fine, I don't want them to think I'm even weirder," I huff, spotting Mum waiting for me by the car.

"Relax, it will be fine, we'll make sure you come across very boring and normal." He hesitates. "Now, which form would you like me to take as your pretend pet tomorrow, a crocodile or a rhino?"

"I've been reading up about witches."

Owen and I both snap our heads up at Iris's statement before sharing a concerned look. Iris doesn't notice our sudden reaction. She's lying across my sitting room sofa, staring up at the ceiling and twirling her hairband round her fingers absent-mindedly.

"Why would you be reading about witches?" I laugh nervously. "The presentation is supposed to be about the Tudors."

"Did you know that witches have familiars?" she asks, ignoring me, still in her own world.

Owen and I both instinctively glance at Merlin, who is in his black cat form, snoozing in the middle of the floor in a warm patch of sunlight streaming in through the window.

"Back in the seventeenth century, they even made a law about it," she continues. "According to the Witchcraft Act of the time, it was illegal to have one. I've read that familiars are 'demonic companions'. Isn't that cool? Imagine having a demonic familiar with you all the time."

"Sounds . . . stupid," Owen says, clearing his throat.

"Yeah, really stupid," I agree. "Do you know what is not stupid and actually very interesting? Two of Henry VIII's wives were related. Catherine Howard and Anne Boleyn were cousins! I think I might do my presentation on Catherine Howard."

Iris's growing interest in witches is making me very nervous. We don't have many magical items lying around the house just in case we have any surprise visitors, but I'd been extra careful to check that there was nothing left on show that could be construed as witch-like. I'd even used a spell to create a spider hutch that I'd put up in my bedroom in case Iris wanted to see my room and wondered where my infamous tarantula was kept.

I might be paranoid, but I'd noticed that when Iris arrived, she was strangely curious about my family, asking me a LOT of questions about Mum and what she did, examining all the books on the shelves and the trinkets up on the mantelpiece. It was almost as if she was looking for something.

"I wonder how the familiars hide themselves in everyday situations," Iris says, sitting up and moving her laptop off her knees. "People would notice, wouldn't they?"

"Yeah, they would, which is why they can't possibly exist," Owen says, looking at her as though she's lost the plot. "Iris, are you OK? You're talking as though familiars are real."

She smiles at him, raising her eyebrows. "How can you be so sure they're not real? They're magic, Owen. They can disguise themselves in clever ways that we'd never notice."

Did I imagine it or did her eyes flicker at Merlin when she said that?

"You're telling me," Owen sighs, "that you think witches exist?"

"I'm telling you that we can't be *sure* they don't," she says, waggling her finger at him. "Don't you believe in magic, Owen? Just a tiny bit?"

"No, Iris, I do not believe in magic." He grins, before getting to his feet. "I'm going to go grab some more popcorn. Any takers?"

"Yes please!" I say, thrilled to move away from the current topic of conversation. "But make sure—"

"I bring you the sweet popcorn, not salty," Owen says, finishing my sentence for me. "I remember from the ten billion times you've told me that you prefer sweet popcorn."

"Salty popcorn is just wrong."

He laughs and leaves the room. I'm pleased with how well he's handling being on witch territory, acting as though he's comfortable in the house. When he first arrived, he shivered, stepping over the threshold and going, "Eugh. This place gives me the heebie jeebies," but he seems to be taking it in his stride now, happy to go have a nose around the kitchen on his own. I hope he doesn't find the baby photos I stashed in a drawer.

I notice Iris giving me a strange look. She leans in conspiratorially. My whole body tenses; I'm terrified she's going to ask me if I'm a witch.

"What?" I squeak.

"Has he asked you to the dance yet?" she whispers.

I look at her blankly.

"You know, the big dance after the final round of the quiz! Has Owen asked you to be his date?"

"W-what? What are you talking about? No! Course not. Why would he ... what ... why would he ask me?"

She sits back with a smug expression. "Everyone can see it."

"See what?" I frown at her. "Iris, what are you talking about?"

"The spark between you two!"

"WHAT?" I stare at her. "Between me and *Owen*?"

"Oh, come on." She laughs. "It's so obvious. You're always together, talking privately all the time. Sharing secrets..."

"We don't share secrets," I say hurriedly, heat rising to my face as she looks unconvinced. "And we don't have a spark! We're friends!"

"If you say so," she says, folding her arms. "I *bet* that he asks you to the dance. If he does, would you say yes?"

I blink at her, unable to answer her question. I feel MORTIFIED. My whole face feels like it's on fire and my mouth has gone dry. I hadn't even thought about the dance yet and I definitely hadn't considered Owen might ask me as his ... *date*. ARGH. Even the word DATE makes a shiver run down my spine! What does she mean, *everyone can see it*? See what? This spark we supposedly have? *Do* we have a spark? Owen would never actually *like* like me, would he? I'm a witch! He hates witches. How do you know when you have a spark? WHY IS IT SO HOT IN THIS ROOM?

"Would you?" Iris repeats, watching me curiously.

I think about her question, my brain frazzled from all this craziness.

Would I say yes if Owen asked me to the dance?

Suddenly, Merlin jumps to his feet and pounces on my lap, claws out, looking me directly in the eye and hissing loudly.

"Whoa!" Iris says, recoiling. "What's wrong with your cat?"

He's worried about what I'm going to say. He's telling me off for even considering it.

"He's very stupid," I say, attempting to push Merlin off me, but he's sunk his claws into my trousers and is holding fast. "He does this sometimes."

"He looks possessed," she remarks as Merlin continues to hiss at me, baring his teeth. Iris gasps, her eyes widening. "Like a demon!"

"Ha ha ha," I say drily, before giving Merlin a warning look and giving him a pat on the head. "All right, kitty, calm down. There's a good cat."

He refuses to move from my lap, but he does stop hissing. When Owen comes back into the room carrying a large bowl of popcorn, Merlin glares at him.

"Everything OK?" Owen asks, passing me the bowl. "I thought I heard a commotion."

"My cat was being a bit odd," I say in a strained voice. "You know what he's like."

"Yeah, he's a strange one," Owen comments, smiling sweetly at Merlin, revelling in the opportunity to insult him with no fear of a comeback. "Have you decided which Tudor you're going to do the presentation on, Iris?"

Iris opens her mouth to speak, but before she can, the doorbell rings.

"That will probably be Howard again," I sigh. Merlin finally allows me to push him off so I can answer the door.

Howard has misplaced his key to our house and I was getting a little irritated that I had to keep getting up to answer the door when he came to check in on us, but as it now gives me an excuse to unhook Merlin's claws from my legs AND avoid eye contact with Iris, I'm much happier about it.

I leave Owen and Iris in the sitting room, Merlin trotting along next to me. As soon as we get into the hall he purposefully ducks between my feet, making me trip up.

"Hey! What is wrong with you?" I whisper, glaring at him. "Stop acting so strangely in front of Iris, she's getting suspicious."

"You will have NOTHING to do with warlocks," he

replies furiously. "It's bad enough you're friends with one of them, but I will NEVER let you—"

"All right, I get it," I say, rolling my eyes as I get the lock on the door. "Nothing to do with warlocks."

I swing open the door to find a flamboyantly-dressed man on the step. He starts when he sees me.

"Morgan," he breathes, putting a hand on his chest.

"Yes?" I say, looking him up and down, not recognizing him at all.

"Morgan," he repeats, his eyes gleaming with tears. "It's me, Maverick. Your dad."

✦ Fifteen ✦

I'm frozen to the spot. I'm so shocked that I can't seem to remember one word of the English language.

"Mefgh."

That's all I can say. That's it. The first time I meet my dad and that's how I greet him. *Mefgh*.

"Sorry," he says, blinking back tears. "I know this must be a shock."

Merlin, with one paw on my foot, hisses at him in confusion.

Maverick is not what I imagined. He's tall and slender, with a mop of bedraggled fair hair, big green eyes and slightly pronounced front teeth that have a gap in the middle. He's wearing a floral green shirt and black trousers with a long purple overcoat and scuffed brown leather shoes.

To be honest, I'm not exactly sure what I imagined my dad to be like, but I do know I didn't imagine anyone like him.

"May I come in?" he asks, giving me a hopeful smile.

"Uh ... I... C-could you wait one ... one second. Wait here one second, yes," I manage to blurt out, before stepping back and slamming the door shut.

With no one else in the hallway, Merlin is able to transform from cat to moth, flying up to my shoulder, landing and changing into his tarantula form.

"What are we going to do?" he asks desperately.

"I'm not sure," I say, my throat tightened with panic.

Collecting myself, I hurry back to the sitting room and stand in the doorway, trying to act as normal and carefree as possible.

"Was it Howard?" Iris asks, looking up from her laptop.

"Yes," I lie, before clearing my throat. "Owen? Could I borrow you for a moment? I need your help with ... uh ... something."

"Sure," he says, getting up and following me out the room.

Iris raises her eyebrows at me, flashing me a knowing smile, and I want to tell her this is absolutely NOT what she thinks, but I don't have the time for that right now.

"You OK?" Owen asks when we reach the kitchen. "You look stressed. Have you accidentally eaten another bug?"

"No! That was one time! And the bug flew right in my mouth when I was laughing in the park and ... anyway, that doesn't matter right now." I run a hand through my hair and lower my voice to a whisper. "Maverick is outside."

"WHAT?" he cries, before I remind him to keep his voice down. "Are you serious?"

"Yes!"

"Why?"

"I don't know! I didn't invite him!"

"How does he know where you live?"

"When I wrote to him I gave him my address so he could write back!"

"Morgan! You didn't think to give him your email address instead?"

"You told me he was old-school!" I argue in a hushed tone. "And I didn't think he'd just show up unannounced."

His forehead furrows in concentration. "What do you want to do?"

"I don't know," I say, throwing my hands up in the air. "I don't know what to do. He's asked if he can come in. I guess he's come all this way. He says ... he says he *is* my dad."

Owen's expression softens. "Are you OK?"

I nod, looking down at the floor. "Yeah. I'm fine. A bit overwhelmed, but I'm OK. What if Mum comes back and finds him here? Owen, what shall I do?"

"Do you want to speak to him? Or do you want me to tell him to leave?"

I lean back on the kitchen counter and take a deep breath in and out, thinking through my options.

"I don't want him to leave just yet. I want to talk to him."

Owen nods. "Do you want someone here with you? Iris and I can stay, if you want?"

I give him a weak smile. "Thanks, but I should probably do this alone."

"OK, I'll get Iris and we'll go. You can always call if you need to."

"What are you going to say to Iris? She'll see Maverick standing outside when you go. I don't want her to know who he is."

"We'll pretend he's Howard. I'll say we have to go because Felix needs us urgently. Then halfway there, I'll make something up about him changing his mind. Don't worry, we've been here a while, it wouldn't be long until we'd be heading home anyway."

"Thanks, Owen."

He reaches out and grabs me by the shoulders so that I look up at him.

"You've got this," he says simply, before dropping his hands and heading back to the sitting room.

After Owen has delivered a particularly convincing performance, pretending Felix is on the phone demanding Iris and he come meet him, they apologetically gather up their things. I steel myself and open the front door once more to find Maverick patiently waiting on the other side. He stands to attention as Owen and Iris head out, looking mildly confused when Owen deliberately says, "Oh hey, Howard, bye!" as he passes.

I notice Maverick do a double take at Owen, watching him as he walks away. Witches have a sense of another witch being close and I wonder if warlocks have that, too. I would try to probe Maverick about it to make sure it doesn't come out later that there was another warlock in Mum's house, but I figure he'll soon forget about it – both Mum and Maverick will surely have more important things to worry about at their first meeting after all these years.

"I didn't realize you had company," Maverick says, once they're down the road and out of earshot. "I apologize for interrupting."

"Morgan?" Howard's voice suddenly floats over from next door and I wince at the timing.

I hear his front door shut and he appears on our drive, pulled towards us by an eager Puffin.

Howard must have seen the others walking past his house through his front window and come to check on me. If my brain wasn't so boggled at the current situation, I'd be laughing at how over-protective he is. While Iris and Owen were at the house, he knocked on the door three times to check all was OK. I asked him if he'd prefer to come chill at ours so he didn't have to keep pottering over, but he kept putting his hands up and going, "No, no, I know you cool teenagers need your space. I won't get in the way; I'll keep checking in."

He comes to stand next to me in the doorway, eyeing up Maverick very suspiciously as Puffin jumps up to greet him with a big slobbery lick. Maverick laughs, giving him a scratch behind his ear.

"What a pleasant fellow," Maverick comments, as Puffin jumps up at him again. "Now, is this a horse or a dog?"

Howard clears his throat, making it clear that he's in no mood for joking with a stranger who has appeared at my door. "How can we help?"

"I'm here to see Morgan." Maverick hesitates, adding quietly, "And Aggie."

"Do you know this person, Morgan?" Howard asks, his eyebrows knitted together.

"No. Yes. Well, sort of," I say, biting my lip.

"I'm Maverick," he says, holding out his hand. "Morgan's father."

Howard recoils, looking horrified. His expression turns from shock to fury, and he pointedly does not shake Maverick's hand. While Howard doesn't know anything about the magical side of things, he does know that this man walked out on his wife's best friend and her baby. I can imagine he doesn't think much of him.

Howard quickly tugs on Puffin's lead, pulling him away from Maverick.

"Does Aggie know you're here?" Howard asks him, putting a comforting hand on my shoulder.

Maverick drops his hand and, blushing, shakes his head. "Afraid not. I would have called ahead but I didn't have a number and – " he smiles broadly at me – "I recently discovered this is where you were living and I couldn't stay away. Look – " he glances at Howard pleadingly – "I know this is a surprise but might I be able to come in? This all seems a bit odd standing on the doorstep. And it is a bit chilly out here."

"Yes, come in," I say, before Howard can turn him away.

I stand aside to let him in. Howard glares at Maverick

as he walks in, head bowed, wiping his feet on the mat and lurking awkwardly in the hall. Puffin bounds into the house, delighted to be let off the lead so he can go cause havoc. Howard marches in behind him and then turns to face me, asking in a quiet voice, "Are you sure about this, Morgan? I can tell him to leave if you want. You can wait for your mum to come back."

"No, it's OK, thanks, Howard."

He keeps a close eye on Maverick who is busy admiring the few picture frames I left up of Mum and me. I lead him into the kitchen and go about putting the kettle on to make tea.

"I'm going to make a call," Howard says, cutting through the silence and getting his phone from his pocket.

We all know he's calling Mum, so we nod in silence before he disappears into the sitting room.

"Thank you for writing to me," Maverick says, standing awkwardly by the table. "I can't tell you how much it meant when I received your letter."

"Do you take sugar?" I squeak, getting out three mugs.

I've never been good at handling any kind of emotion and wish there were some kind of instructions about how to act when you meet your dad for the first time. I'm trying to handle too many feelings all at once. As I pour the tea from the pot, my hands shake. I feel Merlin pat my shoulder with one of his tarantula legs, just to remind me he's there.

I think it might be the nicest thing he's ever done.

"Three please."

"Three sugars?"

"Yes. I'm trying to cut down."

"How many do you normally have?"

"Five."

"FIVE?" I blink at him. "That is a lot of sugar."

"Terrible, isn't it?" he sighs, pulling out a chair and sitting down. Puffin bounces into the kitchen after having a good sniff around the sitting room and hoovering up any stray popcorn. He sits down happily next to Maverick, his tongue lolling out. "I've always had a sweet tooth. Pudding is my favourite course of a meal. If I could, I'd have pudding for starter, main and ... well ... pudding."

"That's mad." I smile, adding milk to the tea.

"I've always been a bit mad." He grins, gratefully taking the mug I offer him and watching me curiously as I go to sit opposite him. "Funny that you're a redhead."

"Is it?"

"Yes, my mother was," he says wistfully. "You look just like her."

Howard barrels into the room, clutching his mobile. "Aggie is on her way home. She's asked me to stay put until she gets here."

Maverick nods, tensing at the sound of Mum's name. "I imagine she wasn't best pleased to hear about my arrival."

"She was not," Howard growls.

I gulp, nervous about what's going to happen when Mum gets home. I'm going to have to explain that this is all my fault. She's going to be so cross at me. In my defence, SHE was the one who lied in the first place. I should be the one who's cross. I need to stand my ground and stick to my principles. I have a right to know about my dad.

Although, it can be very tricky to stand your ground when it comes to Mum. She's a lot more articulate and reasonable when it comes to arguments.

Last time we had a fight, it was over the fact that I brought home a sick seagull I found on the side of the road. I thought I could nurse it back to health and the seagull would learn to love me and it would be a really sweet story of unlikely friendship that would maybe inspire a Netflix movie one day, but it turned out the seagull was perfectly fine and must have been just chilling when I found it, because when I brought it into the kitchen and plonked it down on the table it instantly took flight, soaring about in a panic, flapping its wings madly and pooping everywhere including on top of Mum's head.

In that instance, I was actually doing a very nice thing, something I quickly pointed out as she cleaned up the mess. But somehow, with Mum's intricate powers of arguing, I ended up apologizing. It still annoys me when I think about it.

For the next fifteen minutes, Howard remains standing, his arms crossed, his eyes firmly on Maverick. Maverick and I attempt small talk because there's not much else we can do when Howard is silently staring Maverick down the entire time. I'm in the middle of making up some rubbish about which shop Mum purchased our interesting teapot from, when we hear the key in the door.

Howard straightens and Maverick jumps to his feet, combing his fingers through his hair. The front door slams and the sound of Mum's heels on the floorboards – she always wears heels – echoes through the silent, anticipating house.

She appears in the doorway. Her eyes widen as she takes in Maverick.

"Hello, Aggie," he says softly.

She marches right past, without acknowledging him, to wrap her arms around me. Puffin jumps up at her, whining, desperate for her attention.

"Are you OK?" she whispers in my ear, doing her best to hold off Puffin.

"Yeah, Mum, I'm fine," I say, hugging her back, feeling she needs the hug more than I do.

"I'll leave you to it," Howard announces, looping Puffin's lead round his head and dragging him out of the kitchen. "You know where we are if you need us, Aggie."

"Thank you, Howard."

As soon as he has left the house, the familiars come into play. Helena, who has been hiding, transforms from a ladybird to a huge leopard, snarling and baring her teeth at Maverick, who stumbles back from her. Merlin, hating Maverick for being a warlock but also aware that he's my dad, turns into a wolf, sitting at my feet and letting out a warning growl every now and then.

"What are you doing here?" Mum rages, turning on Maverick. "How dare you show up unannounced?"

"Mum, wait, this is all my fault," I say hurriedly, getting to my feet. "I wrote to him."

She stares at me, baffled. "You *wrote* to him? How did you—"

"I found the letter he wrote you when he left," I

explain, swallowing the lump in my throat. "It was an accident. I was cleaning up the study after Puffin destroyed it and it fell out of a book. I didn't go snooping; I saw my name and I wondered what it was. I read it."

"The letter," Mum breathes.

"Yeah. I'm so sorry I didn't tell you, but I was trying to get my head round it all and then I managed to track him down. I thought I'd write to him to try to understand and then—"

"I decided to come to you." Maverick finishes my sentence. "She didn't invite me here, Aggie, she asked me to write back. But as soon as I started reading that letter, I knew I had to come find her."

Mum closes her eyes, as though in pain, and I suddenly feel super guilty for putting her through this. I know she shouldn't have lied to me, but it must be very strange for her to see him again after all these years and I don't want her to be hurting. I instinctively reach out and take her hand.

"Sorry for not telling you, Mum."

"Morgan," she says eventually, "I'm the one who should be saying sorry. I could never quite bring myself to tell you that . . . that—"

"My dad is a warlock?" I offer.

She nods, pursing her lips.

"Yeah, it's a lot to take in," I admit.

"We broke every rule in the book," Maverick says, smiling warmly at me. "All worth it, of course. Look at you." He turns to Mum. "Aggie, I can't tell you how happy I was to receive her letter. After all these years, to be given the chance to see her."

"I'm the Great Sorceress, Maverick," Mum hisses as Helena snaps her jaws. "I hardly disappeared into the unknown. I wasn't exactly unreachable; your kind all know of me. If you'd wanted, you could have tracked us down long before now."

"I knew you didn't want me to! But when I got Morgan's letter, it was like receiving permission to reach out to you both."

"So of course you thought you'd just show up!" Mum throws her hands up in the air in exasperation. "Typical Maverick! No thought for anyone else involved, act on every whim. What if someone saw you? A famous warlock showing up here at my house? It's . . . unthinkable! Thank goodness Dora is away this weekend! You need to go."

"I'll go, but Aggie, I want to be a part of her life," he says firmly. "Let me try to make it up to you. Please, both of you, think about it. I'll leave my phone number. I'd love to see you both again soon. Perhaps we could do some fun days out together, get to know each other."

Mum shakes her head at the floor, as Maverick carefully places his card down on the table.

"Sounds good," I say gently, walking round the table and gesturing to the hall. "I'll show you out."

"Thank you," he says, before nodding goodbye to Mum. She can't bring herself to look at him.

I open the front door and he walks out, turning to face me on the front step. Merlin, still in wolf form, fiercely growls to make sure he doesn't think about attempting any sort of hug.

"Morgan, I know you're a witch and, if you're anything like your mother, undoubtedly a spectacular one at that," he says, with a drawn-out sigh. "I know what that means. I've never understood the animosity between witches and warlocks. I appreciate it's difficult, but I hope, one day, you'll come to learn that warlocks aren't all that bad."

"Actually," I say, as I think about Owen, "I happen to already know that."

His mouth twitches into a smile and then, without another word, my dad turns on his heel and walks away from me, his long coat billowing in the breeze.

CHAPTER

Sixteen

Mum has been pacing around the kitchen for the past five minutes.

Which doesn't sound like very long, but when you're sitting there watching her do nothing but pace in silence, it feels like FOR EVER. She looks deep in thought, though, so I don't want to interrupt her. There must be a lot going on in her head right now. Merlin remains in his wolf form, sitting next to me, letting out a disgruntled sigh every now and then.

While Mum paces, I consider how different Mum is to Maverick. I mean, I've only met him once and it's not like I learned very much about him, but it's clear that they're not exactly an obvious match. Maverick seems eccentric and laid-back, compared to Mum, who wears work clothes on holiday. But then, Mum has always been drawn to the opposite of her. Take Dora, for instance. Maybe it's the same with her romantic relationships. Opposites attract and all that.

I've never known Mum's "type" when it comes to dating, because I've never known her to date anyone. I once saw a heartwarming movie about a girl who set her mum up with this charming guy and watching it made me realize that Mum and I had never talked about that kind of stuff. So, when the film ended, I felt the need to find her in her study and tell her that I was perfectly happy with her dating, there was no need for her to hold back on my account.

"Thank you for the permission, Morgan," she'd said, trying not to laugh. "But I have a lot of work on at the moment, so I'm happy not to date for now."

But that was a long time ago and she still hasn't gone out with anyone, not even for one date. She doesn't seem to be interested in finding anyone. I guess it would be quite annoying if she started dating a normal guy. I'd have to actually tidy things away or cook things without clicking my fingers and using magic to do it.

"I'm so sorry, Morgan," Mum says eventually, bringing her pacing to an abrupt halt by leaning on the chair next to me. "You must be very confused. We should talk it out."

She sits down and reaches over to take my hands, looking frazzled.

"Ask me any questions you want," she says, squeezing my hands. "I'll be completely honest. You have my word."

"All right," I say thoughtfully. "I want to know how it all started."

"How what started?"

"You and Maverick. You're a witch. He's a warlock. How did it even happen?"

Mum leans back and runs both hands through her hair, carefully considering her answer.

"It was New Year's Eve and I was in Bath, visiting some friends. There was a big fireworks display on at midnight, but one of the group didn't want to go because he'd just failed an exam and he wasn't feeling up to it. The rest of us managed to persuade him, telling him he'd feel better once he saw all those lights in the sky. We all traipsed to the park and found a good spot. And then the fireworks started."

She pauses, smiling as she remembers.

"They were AWFUL. Honestly, pitiful! I don't know what happened that year, usually they were much better, but whoever organized them had messed up. You have to imagine it, just every now and then this firework would go off and it wouldn't be that impressive and then it would be AGES before the next one was lit. Looking back, it was hilarious, but at the time, our friend was convinced that it was a sign that it was going to be a bad year ahead and he just wanted to go home and go to bed. I couldn't let that happen. It was New Year's Eve! I wanted him to feel uplifted."

She clicks her fingers and two steaming mugs of hot chocolate appear in front of us, mine piled with marshmallows. I take it gratefully, intrigued by her story. She takes a sip of hers and continues.

"When no one was looking, I clicked my fingers and the display became spectacular. Everyone watched on in awe. It was really quite something."

Merlin catches my eye but I glance away, trying to ignore how familiar this story sounds. I know he's thinking the same thing.

"That's when I noticed him," Mum sighs.

"Maverick?" I ask, leaning forward in my seat.

She nods. "He was standing with some friends, staring right at me with this dopey smile on his face. I thought he was a total weirdo at first, so I ignored him, but then later when the display came to a magnificent end, he sidled up to me and said something like, 'Nice magic'. I was stunned, I didn't know what to say! Who was this person? And how did he know about magic? I pretended I didn't know what he was talking about, and he laughed. I thought it was a crazy coincidence and he was just joking about magic. He didn't mention it the rest of the night – he ended up introducing his friends to my friends and we sort of merged groups for the rest of my stay. He didn't tell me that night."

"That he was a warlock?"

"I had no idea. He wasn't famous yet. I don't know how much you know about him, but he's invented a few potions so he's quite well known in warlock circles. He's also known for bending all the rules; the Chief Warlock isn't his biggest fan." She sighs, looking pained. "Anyway, by the end of my few days in Bath, I had fallen for him. That was when he decided to tell me, of course. He always loved to be mysterious and dramatic ... making situations much more complex than they needed to be. If he'd told me from the start..."

She trails off. Helena transforms from a leopard into a white fluffy cat and hops on to her lap for comfort.

"What happened then?"

"I was heartbroken. I told him that we couldn't see each other again. I was furious with him for not telling me before, I mean, what did he expect?" She shakes her head angrily, as though she's back in the moment when this conversation took place all those years ago. "Witches and warlocks are enemies. No question about it. That's how it is." She has another sip of hot chocolate, taking a deep breath to calm herself. "Anyway, we tried to be done with it, but we were young and stupid."

"How long were you together?"

"Almost a year. But it was all very secretive. We couldn't let anyone know. Not even Dora."

"Wait a second." I hold up my hand to stop her. "Dora doesn't know? You tell each other everything!"

Mum shakes her head. "I couldn't tell a soul and neither could he. And then, when he left, I was so ashamed that I'd fallen for his warlock lies that I could never tell anyone the truth. When I moved to Essex with you, Dora assumed your father had been a normal guy and I never corrected her." She looks at me with sadness. "Morgan, I appreciate this is a lot for you to take in, but no one can know about this. If any of the witches found out—"

"You don't need to tell me that, Mum. And you don't need to worry. I won't tell anyone." I hesitate. "What I don't understand is why you lied to me about warlocks."

She frowns. "What do you mean?"

"You always taught me that warlocks are bad."

"Warlocks *are* bad," Mum insists.

"But they can't be if you fell in love with one of them," I point out.

"No, listen to me, Morgan," she says, leaning in with fresh urgency. "Don't you see? Maverick proved it all. Warlocks cannot be trusted. He left us."

"To protect us. That's what he said in the letter."

She snorts. "That's what he wanted us to believe. I thought I could change him, Morgan, but I always knew deep down it wasn't going to last. He was flighty and shallow, always changing his mind and then changing it again, before making some ridiculous, over-the-top gesture. I knew he'd let me down. There is a reason that witches and warlocks cannot tolerate each other – there will always be a power struggle."

"Why?"

"Because warlocks can never comprehend the power of witches." She looks me right in the eye and says in her most serious tone, "Morgan, I may have kept secrets from you about your father, and I apologize for that. But I have never lied to you, not once, about warlocks. They're truly terrible creatures, who will always be jealous of us and power-hungry. That's why we must keep our distance and only help them clean up their mistakes when we have to."

I know I'm not going to get anywhere with this, so I decide to nod along. For now.

"All right, but what are we going to do about Maverick?"

"What do you want to do?" she asks, watching me closely.

"I don't know. Maybe . . . maybe I should give him a chance. We could hang out a bit. It would be nice to get to know him."

Mum tries her best to look understanding, although I can see from her eyes that she's crushed. I get a pang of guilt at her downcast expression, but I don't want to lie to her. I really do want to get to know my dad and I don't want to meet up with him behind her back or anything. Along with my friendship with Owen, it would just be ANOTHER lie I'm telling her. I have to be honest when it comes to Maverick, even if it hurts her feelings.

"Yes, of course you want to get to know your father. Thing is, I don't want him to hurt you. I know Maverick. He's magnetic and charming, but he's also selfish and ambitious. In a few days, he might change his mind and what will happen then? Do we trust him? He could have found you long before now if he really wanted to be in your life, as he says he does."

"We'll never know if we don't try," I point out. "Half term is coming up. I could suggest that we go out for a day or something. See how it goes. Otherwise, I think I'd always wonder. Does that make sense?"

She gives me a sad smile. "Yes, it does. I suppose I can't stop you. I'm so sorry that you have to put up with a warlock for a father. It's unspeakable."

"I don't know," I say, watching her carefully. "I think it's sort of . . . romantic."

She looks startled. "*Romantic?* What on earth are you talking about?"

"It's a classic love story, isn't it?" I offer as she blinks at me. "Romeo-and-Juliet forbidden love stuff."

She shakes her head. "Trust me, Morgan, it was NOT romantic. It was pure stupidity and ignorance, not to mention disrespectful to witches of the past, present and future."

"Do you regret it then?"

"Not for a moment," she says, looking me straight in the eye. "Because otherwise I'd never have had you."

I pause, wondering how to word my next question. "Mum, what do you think I am?"

"I'm sorry?"

"The rule is, if you've got a warlock parent you're a warlock, and if you've got a witch parent, you're a witch. What if you have both?"

Her expression instantly darkens. "You're a witch," she says in a deep, low voice.

"Yes, but—"

"No, Morgan, no buts. I understand why you'd ask, but there have never been any signs of warlock behaviour. You're a witch."

I know from her tone that that is the end of the conversation. It's probably a good thing. I have a headache and for some reason really want to be on my own right now. I stand up, the legs of the chair screeching across our kitchen floor.

"I'm going to go to my room," I say, as Merlin transforms from a wolf to a monkey, hopping up on my shoulder, his tail wrapped around my neck. "I need a little time out."

"Are you sure?" Mum says, jumping to her feet.

"Yeah. It's been a very long day," I say, heading to the stairs without looking back at her, "what with all these spells and secrets."

CHAPTER

✦ Seventeen ✦

Mum and I meet Maverick at the woodland on Monday morning of half term.

He is waiting for us when we get there, waving cheerily as Mum pulls up in the car. He's dressed in orange trousers and a white shirt, with a floor-length emerald-green coat. It seems strange that I would have a father with such a bold, colourful sense of style, when most of the clothes I own are black. Maybe that's a witch thing. Mum turns off the engine and takes a moment to steel herself before opening the door. I hop out of the passenger seat with a mixture of excitement and nerves. I can't believe I'm about to spend a day with my *dad*.

Mum is nervous about leaving me with him for the day, worried he'll do something irresponsible or silly, and we'll get in trouble somehow. But I've promised her we'll just be chatting and hanging out, getting to know each other, that's all, no fuss. When I said that, she looked unconvinced and went, "When it comes to Maverick, there is always fuss. And not in a good way."

She's also terrified that a witch will see us together and discover that Maverick is a warlock, so when she rang Maverick to give him permission to come and spend the day with me, she had one condition: it couldn't be at our house and it couldn't be anywhere too public. There are local witches about – Sandy and her mum, for example – and the risk is too great.

The woodland was my idea. Witches do sometimes come here, but mainly at night when it's empty and they can practise flying without being seen. During the day, there are mostly dog walkers, but as it's still early in the year and quite chilly, it's deserted. I thought we could do a picnic or something, and I've been practising my picnic spells, like summoning delicious sandwiches and scones, and creating a heated shelter should it start raining.

"I'm working from home today, so I will be back here in three hours to pick her up," Mum is telling Maverick sternly as I approach, clutching my backpack straps. "Don't be late."

"We won't be."

"And you're not to go anywhere but this woodland, Maverick, is that clear? If anyone sees my daughter with a warlock—"

"I'll be very careful," he says, holding up his hands.

"You're never careful." She narrows her eyes at him. "Don't do anything stupid."

"I wouldn't dream of it, Aggie."

"I mean it," Mum emphasizes, before turning to me. "Morgan, are you sure you're happy about today? You don't have to do this if you're not feeling ready."

"I'm ready, Mum. It's OK."

"And you have your phone fully charged in case you want to call me to pick you up earlier?"

"I've got a hundred per cent battery and I can always use magic, you know, being a witch." I give her a comforting smile. "Stop worrying, Mum. It will be fine."

Helena in her butterfly form flits near to me. "Merlin, you remember what we talked about?"

"Yes, of course," Merlin says, as a ferret round my neck. "If he doesn't toe the line, I'll kill him."

Maverick looks alarmed.

"What? I don't remember this chat," I say, frowning.

"Not quite what we discussed, but I like where your head is at," Helena says with a nod, flying back to Mum's shoulder.

"We should be getting on if we only get three hours." Maverick jumps in enthusiastically. "I have thirteen years to catch up on."

"You're lucky you get three hours," Mum mutters, before pulling me into a hug, holding me a little longer than usual. "Call me if you need me."

"I'll be fine, Mum," I assure her with a big smile to reiterate my point. "Thanks, though."

"Thank you for this, Aggie," Maverick says in this gentle, sincere tone. "It means a lot to me."

She gives him one last warning look, before marching back to the car. We watch her slide into the driver's seat and pull away, Helena now in the form of a large dog, baring her teeth at Maverick through the passenger window as they disappear into the distance.

"She really is something, isn't she?" Maverick observes, watching her go. "I'd forgotten how intimidating she can be."

"Yeah. Try playing board games with her."

"Do you know what? I remember attempting to take her on at a game of chess. It didn't go well for me. Anyway!" He smiles and claps his hands together, before gesturing for me to follow him down the woodland path. "I'm so happy that you're giving me a chance, Morgan."

"It will be nice to get to know you," I say, falling into step with him.

"I can't believe how grown-up you are." He chuckles, clasping his hands behind his back as we wander towards the trees. "Last time I saw you, you were just a tiny baby. Now look at you, a fully-fledged witch."

Maverick smiles broadly at me and I think he considers giving me a hug because his fingers twitch, but he thinks better of it when Merlin changes into a deadly viper snake, coiled round my neck and snapping in his direction.

"So," Maverick continues. "Are you excited about a day of fun?"

"Sounds great," I say, as Merlin changes from a snake to a wasp, flying along next to me. "Are we going to go for a picnic?"

"Is that what you'd like to do?"

I shrug. "I thought it might be a nice option because we've got to stick to the woodland."

"Oh, we won't be sticking to the woodland." Maverick grins.

"But Mum said—"

"Don't worry, we're not breaking any rules," he assures me, as we step over some logs blocking the path. "We'll stick to the woodland but add a bit of magic. I thought I might take this opportunity to show you what warlocks are capable of."

I smile at him knowingly. "No offence, Maverick, but I don't think you're ever going to be able to convince me that warlocks are as good as witches."

"Is that so?" He grins, chuckling. "Do you want to know the main difference between witches and warlocks?"

"Everyone knows that," I say, twigs crunching beneath my feet. "You're stuck making boring potions while we just click our fingers and get whatever we want right away."

"That is one difference, but the *main* one is imagination."

I shoot him a strange look. "What do you mean?"

"Witches don't have any! That is what I have come to realize. Witches see the world around them and change it to suit them. Warlocks see the bigger picture. For example – " he stops in a clearing and gestures around him – "here we have a nice spot for a picnic, don't you think?"

I glance around and nod. "Sure."

"So a witch might click her fingers and magic a picnic blanket or, if she wanted to go fancier, a delightful picnic table, full of delicious food, yes?"

"That sounds wonderful to me."

"It is wonderful, it's *magical*!" Maverick enthuses.

"But a warlock would see this clearing and think, this is a marvellous spot for an adventure!"

I burst out laughing as he dances around the clearing.

"Life is what you make it, Morgan," he continues, prancing about me. "If there's one thing your father can ever teach you, let it be that."

He stops, digs into his pockets and pulls out a handful of small vials of potion, each a different colour. He opens the palm of his hand and comes towards me.

"Pick one," he says, his eyes twinkling. "Each one is a different adventure. I've made these specially for today."

I admire the potions. They're all so different and intricate. One is a swirling mixture of pink and yellow, another is green with delicate purple bubbles rising to the surface, and one is light grey with dots of blue. The vial that catches my eye is filled with a slowly-swirling potion of rich navy with gold sparkles. I pick it out.

"Ah, you've picked a good one," Maverick tells me, putting the other vials back into his pocket. "Possibly my favourite. It took me a long time to invent this potion and it's *extremely* difficult to get right."

"What is it?" I ask, entranced by the glittering gold.

He grins. "You'll see." He takes the vial from my hand and pulls out the cork, before passing it back. "You need to take at least two gulps."

"If this potion isn't quite right. . ." Merlin begins, with a warning glare at Maverick.

"I wouldn't put you in any danger," Maverick promises me. "I'm just going to open your eyes."

I lift the vial to my lips. As instructed, I take two big gulps and hand the vial back to Maverick, who drinks the rest.

At first, nothing happens.

Then, suddenly, the ground shifts beneath my feet. I desperately attempt to keep my balance as the soil and leaves begin to move. Merlin transforms back into a snake, wrapping himself around my neck.

"Don't worry," Maverick says calmly, beaming at us. "Wait and see."

It's not just the ground changing, but the trees around us too. They begin shaking and, as I look around frantically, I realize that they're starting to . . . *fade*. I look down and the ground is disappearing too, but I'm not falling. I'm perfectly still. The whole woodland around me is disappearing into a dark navy haze. And small dots of gold and silver begin to twinkle around us.

"What is going on?" I ask Maverick anxiously.

"Can't you see it yet?" he says, bemused. "Welcome, Morgan Charmley, to your very own galaxy."

It all begins to come into focus. I can barely breathe

as I gaze around us at the clusters of twinkling stars that go on as far as I can see. I'm somehow standing on nothing, suspended in the middle of space, blinking in awe at the billions of lights.

Maverick chuckles at my expression. "Well, what do you think?"

"It's so beautiful," I whisper, reluctant to disturb the tranquillity.

"I bet you've never walked amongst stars before," he says, strolling around, admiring a nearby glowing star.

"How ... how have you done this?"

"You're still in the woodland," he tells me, sitting down on nothing, seemingly floating. "We're still in that clearing. It's a spell that makes us see what it's like to be up there. It took me years to perfect this kind of magic," he says, dreamily looking above him. "But it was all worth it. It's really quite something."

I go to take a step towards him, lifting my foot and pointing it out in front of me before carefully stepping down. I don't fall forwards; there is somehow ground beneath me, though I can't see it. I take another step, grinning as I start to get used to walking on air. I come to sit down next to him.

"It's a nice way to escape," Maverick admits. "When the world gets too much, I come here."

"I'm not surprised. I wouldn't want to leave. It's so peaceful. This is beautiful magic."

"I know this is only the start, but have I changed your mind on warlocks at all?"

"For a warlock, this magic is pretty cool," I say, making him laugh. "I've always thought it must be tiring learning all the ingredients and recipes for potions."

"It is, but it's worth it for moments like these."

"What's the best potion you've ever made?"

"You can't ask me that!" he cries, leaning back on his hands and stretching his legs out in front of him, a star twinkling just by his feet. "There are too many to choose from. But I can tell you one of the worst ones I've ever attempted. I was at school and had been given the usual warning from my mother not to use any potions during the day. I was quite good at sticking to that rule in general. Anyway, I don't know about you but I'm useless at sports. . ."

"Me too!"

"You may get that from me, I'm afraid." He chuckles, shaking his head. "It never was my thing. And this one boy, Derek Terry, always made fun of me. He said I ran like a giraffe: all limbs, no style. Any chance he had to point out that I was a big freak, he took it."

"Sounds like someone I know."

"I thought I'd show him by taking some potion that would make me the fastest runner in the school. I'd read about this brilliant one that gave you the speed of a cheetah," he recalls, running a hand through his hair and making it all stick up. "I stayed up late making it as carefully as possible, because it was a complicated recipe. The next day, I took it right before running class and..."

He grimaces.

"What happened?" I ask eagerly.

"Next thing I knew ... I had the legs of a cheetah! Furry all over!"

"No!"

"Yes," he says, burying his face in his hands at the memory. "I still remember the pain as my legs changed into actual cheetah legs! I had to cover them with a towel, making sure it was long enough so no one could see my paws, and then make a telephone call to Mum asking her to come pick me up, before hiding in the cleaning cupboard until she came to get me with an antidote."

"That sounds awful," I say, unable to stop myself from giggling. "I can't believe you actually got cheetah legs!"

"I would not recommend it. My mother was not happy at all, so on top of the pain and humiliation, I was severely punished. I don't think I was allowed to do any magic or learn any potions for a month at least."

"I got in trouble when I turned another witch into a cactus," I admit, still smiling at the idea of him with cheetah legs, like a creature in a Greek myth. "Apparently it took her a few days to get over the trauma."

"A cactus." He looks impressed. "That's very imaginative. I take it you're not friends with this witch?"

"More like enemies," I confirm. "And what's worse is, I'm up against her in this big quiz thing at school, so I have to keep seeing her. We're on opposite teams. We have one more round and then the big final, and I can't imagine losing to her. She'd never let me live it down."

"It sounds like it might be a lot of fun," he says wistfully. "I used to be on the debate team at school, which was similar I imagine. How interesting that you're on your school quiz team."

"Actually, it was an accident. I shouldn't have been on the team at all." I let out a sigh, staring out into the Milky Way. "I'm on the team because of a warlock."

Maverick raises an eyebrow. "Oh?"

I'm not sure why I've told him that. I haven't even spent a day with him and I've already spilled my biggest secret. He did say that he's never really understood the witch-warlock divide himself, and it feels nice to be able to tell someone the truth.

I hope I can trust him. I *want* to trust him.

"Would that be the warlock that was round your house the day I arrived?" he asks.

I nod. "Owen. We're in the same class. Complete coincidence. Somehow we ended up being friends. I can never tell Mum. Ever."

"No, I see that," Maverick says thoughtfully. "Do you want my opinion?"

"Sure."

"I think it's a good thing." He smiles warmly at me. "I believe witches and warlocks can learn a lot from each other. By ourselves, our magic is powerful, but if we worked together – " his eyes widen at the thought – "imagine what we could achieve. Imagine it! There would be no limit. No rules! The divide between the magical folk is outdated and stifling. A centuries-old grudge that no one seems to be able to get over."

"When I think about it, it does seem strange that my friendship with Owen is against the rules. Mum says there will always be a power struggle between witches and warlocks, which makes sense when I think about the warlock stories I've heard—"

"Let me guess," Maverick interrupts, laughing, "warlocks in those stories are arrogant, selfish, power-grabbing folk, with little compassion or kindness."

I smile apologetically. "Something like that."

"And is Owen like that?"

I shake my head. "Not at all. If anything ... if anything, he makes me want to be better. You know, kinder and stuff. I get in trouble a lot and he has to help me out. Sometimes I get a bit carried away and I don't think things through like he does."

"You may get that impulsive streak from me." Maverick chuckles.

"It gets me into plenty of sticky situations. That's why I ended up doing this school quiz. I cast a spell on Owen when he was annoying me, and then as revenge, he gave me an enthusiasm potion the day they were asking for volunteers for the quiz team."

He laughs. "A neat trick. Sounds to me like you and this Owen complement each other."

"We're good friends." I lower my eyes. "Sometimes I feel guilty, though, about being his friend. Mum would be so mad if she ever found out. She wouldn't even give him a chance, I don't think. He's a warlock, so she'd hate him. It's so annoying."

"I've learned to stop caring about what other people think," Maverick says with a wave of his hand. "It's very tiresome. Your mum has to care, it's her job. The witches have put her on a pedestal. She has expectations to live up to. It's not my cup of tea, but everyone must live their life how they wish to. I'm just pleased you're letting me have a glimpse into yours."

We share a smile and fall into thoughtful silence.

"Maverick," I say eventually, "do you want to come to the next round of the quiz? Parents are welcome to watch. There's no pressure or anything; this is all new and you're probably very busy and don't—"

"I'd love to come along," he interrupts, beaming at me. "I'd love to. That is, if your mother wouldn't mind?"

"I'll check with her. It may not work if Sandy's mum is going to be in the audience. She might recognize a famous warlock. And you don't exactly blend in with the other parents."

He chuckles. "Now, why on EARTH would anyone ever want to blend in? But don't worry, I have a knack for disguise potions. I can show up as someone else."

"That sounds like a good plan to me."

"Marvellous. That would be really marvellous." He reaches into his pocket again and pulls out all the vials that are left. "Right. Ready for the next adventure?"

I smile, selecting the pink and yellow swirled one and pulling out the cork. "I'm ready."

CHAPTER

✦ Eighteen ✦

A few weeks later, Maverick makes an announcement.

"We're going on a field trip today."

"But we're not supposed to leave the woods," I remind him as we reach our usual clearing.

"Aren't you a bit tired of the woods?" he sighs, gesturing around him at the trees. "Sometimes, Morgan, rules must be broken. Otherwise, we'd all go mad."

I share a concerned look with Merlin, who has chosen to take the subtle form of a tiger. We turn our attention back to Maverick, who is now examining the vials in the palm of his hand and smiling to himself as he selects two of them, shoving the rest back in the oversized pockets of his sky-blue coat.

Spending time with Maverick has been truly magical.

Since the first day of adventures in half term, he's visited several times after school and weekends, and each time has been better than the last. I had no idea that warlocks could be so powerful. Through his potions, I've been to the middle of a jungle and seen all the wonders of the world without leaving an Essex woodland, just by taking a few sips.

To be honest, some of the potions taste GROSS. There is one that makes you the funniest person on the planet for ten minutes and I swear, it tasted like liquid Brussels sprouts. I may have made Maverick cry with laughter at my brilliant jokes, but I'm honestly not sure it was worth it.

Mum's been asking a lot of questions about what Maverick gets up to, and I'm trying to be as honest as possible. I wasn't sure at first how happy she'd be about me trying warlock potions, but she didn't seem at all surprised when I'd admitted to sitting in the middle of a galaxy on the first day I spent with him.

"Yes, I remember that one," she'd said, making me a hot chocolate. "It is, admittedly, impressive, but nothing that a witch couldn't do."

With that, she'd clicked her fingers and suddenly I was standing in the galaxy of stars drinking hot chocolate. I'd been so surprised, I'd jumped, spilling my drink over an unsuspecting star.

"Wow, Mum!" I'd gasped. "How come you haven't done this before?"

She'd clicked her fingers again and the vision had disappeared, the twinkling galaxy fizzling away back into our kitchen.

"Because I don't feel the need to show off the extent of my powers," she'd muttered. "Unlike *some* people. Let me guess, he told you that witches have little imagination?"

"Something along those lines."

"Oh, Maverick, still up to the same old tricks," she'd tutted. "Be careful, Morgan. I understand that your father's magic can be hard to step away from, so I'm not going to say you can't go along with it and try a few potions here and there. But my only rule is, you do not leave the safety of that woodland. Got it?"

"Got it," I'd promised.

Now, as Maverick steps towards me excitedly, his hand outstretched, I do my best to stick to that promise.

"We can't leave the woodland," I repeat firmly, attempting to convince myself as much as him. "I promised Mum we wouldn't."

"The only reason your mum doesn't want you leaving the woodland is because she's worried someone might see you with a warlock, yes?"

"I suppose."

"And I understand that," he says solemnly. "She is, after all, the Great Sorceress. I appreciate that it matters to *her* what people think. But—"

"You really don't care what people think?" I interrupt curiously. "You wouldn't mind if a fellow warlock saw you with a witch?"

"Not really," he says breezily, before raising an eyebrow at me. "I've told you this before. You look as though you find it hard to believe."

"Well, only because of the letter," I say, shifting uncomfortably. "The one you wrote Mum when I was a baby. The reason you left. . ."

I trail off and, as his face falls, I wish I hadn't brought it up at all. We've been having such a lovely time together, I don't know why I had to go and make things serious.

"Sorry," I say hurriedly. "It's not important."

"No, it is important," he says, putting up his hand. "The truth is, I wasn't doing that for me, Morgan. As I've said, your mum needs to care what people think because of the position she holds." He gets a dreamy look on his face. "Your mum has always been ambitious, and back then, she knew she was going to become the Great Sorceress one day. If I had stuck around, she would have been an outcast. She'd never have achieved her dream."

"I wish she was a bit more like you and didn't worry

about what everyone else thinks all the time," I say, looking at the ground. "Maybe if she didn't, she'd come join us on our adventures. And we could all be together. She's so careful and cautious with her magic. It sucks that she can't do what she wants because of what other witches might think."

"Morgan," Maverick says, placing a hand on my shoulder and bending down to look me in the eye, "we have to understand that she's in a position of responsibility. We cannot be upset with her for taking all that seriously. The Great Sorceress has to play by the rules. BUT – " he holds out the vials again, his eyes twinkling – "that doesn't mean we have to."

"I don't like any of this," Merlin growls.

"What are they?" I ask, examining the swirling, glittering silver potion in one vial and the pale blue liquid with flecks of white in the other.

"As I was saying, the reason your mum doesn't want us leaving the woodland is because she doesn't want us to be seen, so I've come up with a very clever plan – if I do say so myself – to make sure that we won't be." He pauses for dramatic effect. "The other day, you mentioned that it must be difficult for warlocks to know that witches can fly on broomsticks."

"Yeah." I nod smugly. "That must be rubbish."

He chuckles, shaking his head, before taking the corks out of the vials and handing them over to me.

"Two glugs of the silver first, then three of the blue."

Ignoring the glare from Merlin, I follow Maverick's instructions before handing the vials back to him so he can finish them off. The silver one tastes like custard creams and the blue one like sherbet. The sourness makes my face scrunch up and my eyes water. I wait for something to happen, for the world to begin to spin around us or drift into a different background, but there's nothing. I look to Maverick and gasp. His arms and legs are beginning to vanish into thin air.

"What's happening?" I cry, pointing at him.

That's when I notice that my own arm and hand have disappeared.

"ARGH!"

"Invisibility potion," Merlin says, unable to keep the awe out of his voice. He turns into a small sparrow and flits up to take a closer look at my face. "Very intricate magic."

"This is so WEIRD," I whisper, as I completely disappear.

My insides start to feel warm and tingly, and suddenly my feet lift up from the ground.

"M-Maverick," I croak, as I begin to float upwards. "What's happening? I can't see you!"

"I'm here," he says, and I feel him take my hand in his. "How do you feel about flying to London?"

I glance about madly as we continue to float up through the air, now level with the tree branches. "H-how is this . . . w-what is—"

"The silver potion was invisibility and the blue one gives you the ability to fly. No broomstick needed. And we can leave the woodland without being seen. So, your mum's reputation is safe. You see? I've thought of everything."

"It's impossible," I gasp, holding on to his hand tightly as we drift above the trees, Merlin flying as close as possible to my head, his beady eyes wide and panicked. "You can't just . . . fly!"

"You'll find, Morgan, that there's very little I can't do." He laughs. "And on the rare occasion I discover things I can't do, I jolly well make sure I soon can! The ingredients for flying potion are rare and near impossible to get your hands on, and the spell to make the potion itself takes weeks. There is no room for error. Lucky for you, your dad is rather good at it. You can relax and enjoy it. You're perfectly safe."

"I can't believe this. It's . . . *wonderful*."

It is the most magical, incredible feeling. It is different to being on a broomstick somehow. On a broomstick, I have to focus on a hundred things – controlling the broomstick, balance and speed – whereas I feel like I don't have to think about anything with this potion.

"I'll hold on to your hand so I don't lose you with the invisibility," Maverick says. "Let's go see some sights, shall we? Wait until you see the views from the rooftops."

"Morgan, are you sure about this?" Merlin asks hurriedly. "I'm not exactly one to follow rules myself, but this does seem extreme. If your mum finds out..."

"She won't. How can she?" I say in a daze, as we hover above the woodland. I can see for miles. "I'm sure about this. Maverick, let's go."

"That's my girl!" he exclaims and my heart swells with pride.

Gripping my hand tightly, he leads the way through the air. I hold out my arms like I'm Peter Pan, soaring above the trees, not having to worry about controlling a broomstick, just enjoying the feeling of flying. It's an adrenaline rush like no other. At one point, Maverick asks if I'd like a break, to stop and sit on a rooftop and have a look around, but I tell him I don't want to stop now, not ever. I want to keep on flying. He laughs and on we go, soaring over villages and towns, Merlin flying next to me, everyone below completely oblivious to the two people flying right over their heads. We fly over cows and sheep and horses grazing, over busy motorways and train tracks, until I realize that we're in a very built-up area that's starting to look more and more like...

"London!" I gasp.

"Time for a break," I hear Maverick declare. "We'll go to my favourite spot. It's got a great view."

"You're joking," I say as we come in to land on the roof of Big Ben. I gaze out across central London, taking in breathtaking views of the buzzing banks of the Thames, the Houses of Parliament and Buckingham Palace. "Is this really happening? This isn't just a vision in the woods?"

"This is real," Maverick assures me. I still can't see him and he's let go of my hand now we're sitting on the roof tiles, but I know he's right next to me.

"This is amazing! Mum would never let me do stuff like this! Why don't we do this kind of thing every day?!"

Maverick laughs, but doesn't answer my question. I think he doesn't want to make Mum look bad, but it's impossible for me not to feel as though all the rules that witches follow are a little bit ridiculous. Especially when it comes to being so set on hating warlocks. With their magic, we have the ability to FLY! Who knows if witches can do this kind of magic? And if Mum could do this, she probably wouldn't. Why? Because those are the rules.

"Rules are stupid," I state out loud.

"My feelings exactly," Maverick sighs.

"If I want to be friends with a warlock, I can be."

"I agree."

"If I want to become invisible and fly around London, then I can!"

"Yes." He chuckles. "Although, I wouldn't attempt this kind of magic quite yet, Morgan. It can go very wrong."

I bring my knees to my chest and hug them, watching the people below, little dots rushing about on their way somewhere.

"Morgan, may I ask you a question?" Maverick says suddenly.

"Sure."

"Have you ... have you ever wondered about your warlock side?"

I frown. "My warlock side?"

"Yes. After all, you're part witch, part warlock."

Merlin bristles next to me, furious at the suggestion.

"I think I'm just a witch," I say honestly. "That's what Mum says."

"Yes, well, typical! No imagination." I hear him tut disapprovingly. "There is little doubt in my mind, Morgan, that you are much more than just a witch. I believe that you may be a lot more powerful than that."

I snort. "No chance. That's very nice of you to say, but I'm not even a very good witch."

"What makes you say that?"

"I failed my YWE so many times, it was embarrassing," I explain, feeling my cheeks go hot just at the memories of all those times my mum had to announce I'd failed yet again. "I couldn't control my spells."

"That only serves as further proof," he says enthusiastically, as I frown in confusion. "Why do you think your magic is hard to control? Because you have been gifted both witch and warlock abilities. You are special, Morgan."

"I'm *really* not."

"I've been thinking about what you told me about your adventures last term," he continues, ignoring my protests. "Sounds to me like you cast some extremely powerful spells. So powerful that you couldn't stop them. The bats that turned into dragons. The never-ending salsa dancing. Do you know how hard it is to cast spells like that?"

"I couldn't stop them because the spells were out of control! Not because they were powerful."

"What did everyone else think?"

"What do you mean?"

"Your mum and her friend, Dora. And your friend,

Owen. What did they say? Did they agree that the spells were badly done?"

I think back to the end of last term. Mum was angry about the dragons, but she was also impressed. She said that any witch good enough to summon such magical creatures could get rid of them, and then I did, which was quite advanced magic. I hadn't been taught any of it. The spells came to me naturally. And I remember Owen crouching next to me behind the hedge at Felix's house when the mini dragons sat in the tree, breathing fireballs at us. I remember what he said to me as he looked me right in the eyes: *I think it's clear that you are a very powerful witch, Morgan Charmley.*

I smile at the memory.

"I take it by your silence that I'm not the only one who thinks you're more than you believe," Maverick says. "Tell me, Morgan, have you ever tried making a potion? Ever tried reading a warlock spell book?"

"Of course she hasn't!" Merlin spits, answering before I can. "A witch would never stoop so low."

"When we get back, I'm going to give you one of my books. I want you to have a look at it. It's not one of my published books – it's one I've put together of my favourite potions. Some of them are basic, some of them are very intricate. I want to see what you can do."

"Aggie will not allow such a book in her house," Merlin says.

"I'm not asking Aggie for her permission. I'm asking Morgan," Maverick replies simply. "Will you let me give you the book at least? You don't have to open it until you feel ready."

I bite my lip nervously. I know Mum would kill me if she found out. I know it's against all the rules. But haven't I just declared that rules are stupid? And I can't pretend that I'm not curious. Maverick has shown me that warlock magic is just as cool as the witch kind. Owen has shown me that warlocks aren't evil and cunning.

"I'd like to take a look at the book," I say determinedly. "Thank you."

"Wonderful!" Maverick exclaims. "Just imagine it, someone with the powers of both a witch and a warlock. It would be . . . *extraordinary*."

"It would be disastrous," Merlin mutters angrily.

We sit in silence for a few moments as I let Maverick's words sink in. I don't feel special. In fact, I feel the opposite. It's hard to live up to being the daughter of two exceptionally brilliant magical beings. My mum is the Great Sorceress, a leader of witches. My dad is a genius warlock, famous for inventing spells.

I failed my magical exams countless times and last week I walked into a door.

"We need to go back," Maverick says eventually, reaching for my hand and finding it.

"Why? We just got here!"

"It takes time to go back and forth, and we're on a strict time limit with your mum. I don't want to miss our curfew. Not to mention the invisibility potion wears off in an hour or so."

"Just one more minute," I plead.

"All right, then."

I look out across the London skyline, breathing deeply, taking in as many details as possible. I don't want to forget any of this.

"Thank you," I say after a few moments, when I know I can't delay going home any longer. "Thank you for showing me all this."

"This is simply the start. Magic can take you anywhere."

Mum is furious. And I mean, *furious.*

Maverick and I appear at the edge of the woods where she is waiting by the car, and as soon as she sees me, her expression clouds over, her eyes narrowing to slits as she turns to Maverick.

"How could you?" she hisses at him. "You took her flying! I can see it in her eyes. Tell me you did not go to London!"

Seriously. *How do mums always know?*

"Aggie, we used invisibility potion," Maverick replies, looking unfazed and not even bothering to deny it. "No one saw a thing. We had a wonderful day."

"Morgan, get in the car," Mum instructs, pointing to it.

Grimacing at her angry tone, I say goodbye to Maverick, then hurry over to the car and hop in the passenger seat. I guess I'll have to wait until next time for Maverick to give me the book he talked about.

"You're in BIG trouble," Merlin whispers, transforming into a bat on my shoulder and wrapping his wings around himself. We watch Mum have a heated conversation with Maverick, none of which we can hear, before she storms back to the car.

She doesn't say a word the whole drive home. I can tell she's in deep concentration, because her eyebrows are furrowed and her lips are so tightly shut, they've all but disappeared. I consider apologizing, but I'm not sure if it's me she's mad at, or Maverick, so I keep my fingers crossed that I may be in the clear.

Unsurprisingly, I'm not.

"You promised me one thing," she says as soon as we're in the house. "You promised you would not leave that woodland."

"Mum, we were invisible! It's not a big deal!"

Her eyes go all wide at that comment and she marches into the kitchen, bristling, snapping her fingers to get a cup of tea. I follow her in apprehensively.

"It was hugely irresponsible," Mum says, rounding on me. "Stupid, reckless, thoughtless. Everything you'd expect from Maverick, not what I'd expect from you! Do you know the risks you took today? If the magic had gone wrong?"

"The magic wouldn't go wrong," I say, getting riled up. "Maverick is brilliant! His books on potions are bestsellers. He's invented loads, all the best ones. He doesn't make mistakes."

"Everyone makes mistakes," she argues, throwing her hands up as her cup of tea floats next to her, dodging out of the way of her dramatic gesture. "Maverick is very good at dazzling with his magic, but he doesn't know when to stop! He has never known when to stop. What if something had happened to you today? If you'd been hurt? I wouldn't have known where you were! Maverick only cares about what *he* wants and nothing else."

"Why is it so bad to do your own thing?" I say, raising

my voice in exasperation. "Why do you care so much about the rules and what other witches think?"

"Because the rules keep us safe! They protect us and our magic! Maverick is *dangerous*. When it comes to what's important—"

"The rules keep *you* safe," I point out.

"What do you mean, Morgan?"

"The only reason you don't want Maverick to show me all this cool magic is to protect your reputation as the Great Sorceress!"

She blinks at me, stunned into silence.

"But I'm having fun," I continue. "And you can't stop me from—"

"Your necklace," she interrupts.

During the argument, my necklace has somehow fallen out from behind my jumper and the black pendant is now on full display. I realize it wasn't my words that shocked her into silence, it was the sight of the pendant.

"You've been spending time with a warlock," Mum croaks, looking as though she's struggling to breathe.

"What? Yeah, obviously, I just spent the day with Maverick," I say, confused. "Mum, are you OK?"

"No," she snaps, pained. "Not Maverick. Another warlock."

"Mum, what are you—"

"The necklace is a warning." Her eyes flash at me. "That pendant turns black when the witch wearing it is *falling for a warlock.*"

✦ Nineteen ✦

"W-what? What are you talking about?"

"Do you remember how that piece of jewellery came to be in our family?" Mum asks, giving a sharp nod to the pendant hanging round my neck.

"Yes, you told me that a warlock gave it to my great grandmother," I say quietly, swallowing a lump in my throat, heat rising to my cheeks. "He was in love with her."

"That's right. The necklace is magical. There's a potion swirling inside that pendant. A very powerful potion. The potion is sapphire-blue, but when a witch wearing it falls for a warlock – " she pauses, looking down at the ground – "it turns black."

I stare at her.

"That's how the warlock knew your great grandmother was lying when she told him she didn't love him back," Mum continues, her voice breaking. "She kept the necklace, passed it down to her daughter, and in time it went back to its beautiful blue. Until I met Maverick."

"Mum—" I begin, trying to get my head round all this.

"When Maverick left, it stayed black for a while until I moved on with my life. I wanted to give it to you when it was the colour it should be." She closes her eyes, agonized by what she's revealing. "And now here you are standing in front of me, and the potion is black. Not light blue, not grey, but jet black. You've got close to a warlock, Morgan, there is no question about it. Who is it?"

Betrayed and angry, she opens her eyes to look at me. I feel numb. My throat is tight. I look down at my shoes, unable to take her scrutinizing gaze any longer. I don't understand. I can't believe I've been wearing a magical necklace this whole time that can somehow read my feelings. How is this possible? I have not fallen for a warlock! The only warlock apart from my dad that I know is. . .

"*Who is it?*" Mum asks again, firmer this time.

"Mum, I am not close with a warlock! This is

ridiculous!" I take the necklace off and hold the pendant in my hand. "This thing must be broken."

"Don't lie to me any more, Morgan," she seethes. "You have disregarded every rule I've given you. You have ignored all my advice! All my teachings! Everything that protects you—"

"Stop saying that!" I explode, feeling overwhelmed and suddenly angry. I shove the necklace into my pocket. "Those rules don't protect us! They're outdated and stupid! Why do we have to hate warlocks? Why are witches so set against them? You fell in love with one once!"

"And look where that got me!" Mum cries, baffled at my outburst. "You have no idea what you're talking about, Morgan. You have no idea what warlocks are really like, what they're capable of. Warlocks cannot be trusted. Warlocks and witches are enemies and it will always be that way! Always!"

"Owen is not my enemy! He's my friend! And I trust him more than anyone!"

The words are out of my mouth before I can stop them. Mum recoils, leaning on the kitchen counter to steady herself. I hear Merlin, in his bat form on my shoulder, groan.

"Who is Owen?" Mum says eventually, in a voice so quiet I barely hear her.

There is no point in hiding the truth from her now. It would take her just a few minutes of sleuthing to discover who it was. All she'd have to do is look through the list of class names and she'd see the one Owen in my school year and recognize his surname. All witches know that a warlock owns Blaze Books. That's why Dora was so upset with me last year when I wandered in there, oblivious to the magical family I was about to meet.

"Owen Blaze is in my class at school," I say, my heart thudding against my chest as I watch her reaction closely.

Her eyes widen in horror. "Owen Blaze. *Blaze*."

"Yes."

"How did I miss this?" she says, burying her head in her hands. "Owen Blaze. I know that warlock family is local, but I didn't know the son was in your class." Her expression darkens as she returns her attention to me. "How long have you known he was a warlock? How close are you two? Are you . . . falling for him?"

"ARGH! What?! Look, Mum, I don't know what's wrong with this necklace, but we're just *friends*!"

"The necklace doesn't lie, Morgan. It's *magic*," she hisses. "It tells the truth and only the truth! You can NEVER see this Owen Blaze boy again."

"Mum—"

"How could you keep this from me? The daughter of

the Great Sorceress spending time with a warlock!" She shakes her head in disbelief. "If anyone were to find out!"

"Why is that all you care about?" I yell, clenching my fists. "Why don't you care about me and about how I feel?"

Her face falls. "Morgan, of course I care. But surely you can understand that you have to end your friendship with a *warlock*."

"All you care about is being the Great Sorceress! You're trapped by all the rules and your stupid high status. Well, you can't stop me from being friends with him," I declare, the rage bubbling through me and bringing me a newfound confidence to stand up to my mum. "He's the only person at school who likes me. He's not cunning or power-hungry, or anything else you've told me about warlocks. He's a good friend. Maverick agrees."

Mum gasps, clutching her throat. "You've told *Maverick* about him?"

"Yes. And you know what he thinks? That I can be friends with whoever I want to be friends with, because he's not stuck in the Dark Ages! He's proud of his magic! He celebrates it."

"Maverick is a menace," Mum retorts. "He doesn't care about anyone but himself."

"He cares about me! He's opened my eyes to warlock

magic. He thinks that I might be able to do potions. He thinks I could be powerful. And to be honest, Mum, right now, I feel much more like a warlock than a witch."

She looks winded, as though I've knocked all the breath out of her. I knew that statement would hurt. That's why I said it.

When she just stands there, lost for words, I turn on my heel and march towards the front door.

"Where are you going?" Mum calls out, following me.

"Away from here. I need to be around someone I trust."

"Morgan, I forbid you to go see Owen! Morgan!"

I ignore her and slam the door behind me before running as fast as I can away from home.

Maverick finds me curled up on a plush velvet armchair in the middle of the woodland. I'm pleased to see him. I've had to put up with Merlin droning on at me for half an hour about how I'm losing my mind for even considering any of this "warlock nonsense".

I don't know why he's so cross. I've pointed out to him several times that surely if I could do warlock spells too, that would make me a lot more powerful than most witches. But he's not sure. The idea of being a familiar to someone who is not pure witch is

223

too difficult for him to process. It's ingrained in him to hate warlocks. He's not too happy that I chose to call Maverick in my time of need, but I've already explained there's no one else I can talk to. I can't tell Dora about the fight because then she'd find out about Mum and Maverick. And I'd feel bad bringing Owen into all of this. I'm not ready to tell him that Mum's found out about our friendship.

And the whole necklace angle is making my head hurt. I'd feel nervous around him.

"What happened?" Maverick asks gently.

I click my fingers and a matching armchair appears next to mine. He smiles at the magic and comes to sit down.

"We had a big fight."

"About our adventure today? I'll talk to her. It wasn't your fault."

"No, not about that," I say, leaning back into the squishy cushions. "About Owen. She found out about him."

"Hmm." He nods, not looking surprised. "The necklace?"

I blink at him. "You know about that?"

"Of course," he says, giving me a sad smile. "It was black when Aggie and I were together. She told me it was

228

supposed to be blue. When you told me about Owen, I noticed the familiar black pendant round your neck."

"He's just a friend," I say hurriedly, my face growing hot. "And you should have told me about the necklace. I could have hidden it better if I knew what it meant."

"It wasn't my place to jump in and tell you family secrets." He tilts his head at me. "You've taken the necklace off, I see. I hope you haven't thrown it away. It's a lovely bit of magic."

I reach for it in my pocket and pull it out, holding the top of the chain and letting the jet-black pendant dangle in front of me.

"I don't know what to do with it now. I can't wear it."

He frowns. "Why ever not?"

"Because of what it symbolizes!" I say, baffled that I'm having to justify it. "Mum will probably take it away from me anyway. I've never seen her so mad."

"You shouldn't think like that," Maverick insists. "That necklace belongs to you. It's nice to know that you carry some warlock magic around with you wherever you go."

I hesitate and then realize he's right. I love this necklace. I feel weird not wearing it. I put it back round my neck and fasten the clasp, before tucking the pendant into my jumper.

"I don't know what to do," I say quietly.

"What do you mean?"

"About Owen. And about Mum. She says I can't see him again."

"More rules." He shakes his head. "This is why I've chosen to disregard most of them. You always feel like you're disappointing someone. It will be all right, Morgan, just do whatever it is you want to do. Anyway, I've brought you something."

As he reaches into the inside pocket of his coat, I can't help but feel a rush of irritation at his brushing such a huge dilemma under the carpet. Maybe I need to follow in his footsteps and the only thing I should take seriously is magic. It seems to be working out for him.

"Here."

He holds out a sparkly leatherbound book with a beautiful stars-and-moon pattern on the cover. The title reads, *MOONSHINE'S PERFECT POTIONS*. I smile up at him.

"This is so cool, thank you. Did you say this isn't even published yet?"

"I don't plan on ever publishing that," he tells me with a mischievous grin. "It's simply a collection of the potions I hold dearest to my heart. Don't worry though, it's not my only copy. You can keep that one."

"Wow. Thank you."

He leans back in the chair, his eyes twinkling with excitement. "I wonder what you can do. I wonder about the extent of your magic."

"I wouldn't get your hopes up."

"Well, keep me informed," he says sternly. "If you can do these potions, then we may be on to something huge."

"OK," I say, putting the book down. "In the meantime, what should I do about Owen?"

"That's entirely up to you," he says, tapping his fingers impatiently on the arm of the chair. "I suppose you need to ask yourself a very important question."

"What's that?"

"Your mum is not going to make this easy. She's the Great Sorceress. If you defy her, there will be a storm coming your way." He leans forward, clasping his hands together and holding my gaze. "So, the question you need to ask yourself is this: is your friendship with Owen Blaze worth the risk?"

CHAPTER

Twenty

Mum and I aren't speaking.

When I got home the other night after our fight, she'd been waiting for me in the kitchen. I had stormed up to my bedroom, refusing to acknowledge her. Seconds later I'd heard her footsteps on the stairs, and Merlin and I had braced ourselves for another round of arguing. But that didn't happen. Instead, she'd opened my door – without knocking, I might add, which is just RUDE – and leaned on the doorframe.

"You will end your friendship with Owen Blaze, or I will tell his mother."

"Yeah, sure," I'd snorted. "Like you're going to willingly go talk to a warlock and admit your daughter's been hanging out with her son."

She'd pursed her lips, her expression thunderous. But her voice was calm and controlled. "Watch the attitude, Morgan," she'd said. "And I can promise you, I would have no qualms in telling a warlock to keep her child away from mine. If you don't stop being friends with him, I'll have no choice but to change your school. Goodnight."

Then she'd left. That was it. Her word was final.

Well, I don't care. Maverick wouldn't listen if someone tried to boss him around. He'd just laugh and then carry on doing his thing. That's what I need to do. I need to stop feeling so guilty for going against Mum's silly rules and recognize that I can make my own decisions. I need to be less worried and more carefree. Less timid and more confident.

I need to be less Morgan and more Maverick.

I finally found the courage to fill Owen in on what had happened. I didn't tell him straight away because I thought he might be cross at me, but he wasn't. The only thing he was concerned about was how best to keep our friendship secret. He didn't even consider any other option.

I haven't said a word about the necklace. For obvious reasons.

"Mum is acting normal," Owen informs me quietly on the bus to Woodvale for the third round of the quiz. "She doesn't know anything."

I breathe a sigh of relief. I broke my silent treatment towards Mum for a brief moment yesterday morning to tell her that I had decided to agree to her terms. I didn't want to change schools, so I promised to stop my friendship with Owen.

"You're making the right decision, Morgan," she'd said, beaming at me. "I know it's hard. But it's the right thing to do."

She'd stood up to give me a hug, but I'd backed away from her, and left the house to get the bus to school. I didn't want her to think everything was OK, because it wasn't.

And I was, of course, lying through my teeth.

It was Owen's idea and a smart one at that. I don't know why I didn't think of it. Just agree to her terms, he'd said, and we'll be secret friends. That way Mum wouldn't tell his mum or send me to a different school. Win-win. It's not like Mum can watch me every day at school or anything. How will she know who I'm hanging out with?

Witches have been known to use spies before – usually birds, specifically crows or ravens, sometimes owls depending on the time of day – so Owen and I keep our distance outside the school building in case any beady-eyed birds are watching and reporting back.

I like to think Mum trusts me and wouldn't spy on me.

Although I am completely breaking that trust so, to be honest, I'm not sure who would be in the right or the wrong here.

"Have you had a chance to look at the potion book yet?" Owen whispers eagerly.

"Not yet. Thank you again for lending me that cauldron, by the way."

"No worries, you can keep it. It was my first ever one. It's a good size for beginners."

"Thanks. And it's really nice of you to offer to be there when I try my first potion. I'll need all the guidance I can get. When do you think we should try?"

"It's going to be tricky. We need to make sure our mums are nowhere near and I'm guessing your mum is going to be even more suspicious of who you hang out with now. But don't worry, we'll find a time to meet."

"Maybe the woods at midnight?" I suggest brightly. "They're very dark and spooky, so quite suitable."

"Maybe somewhere less creepy." He shudders. "Witches are so weird."

"It makes me nervous, you know, the idea of making potions," I say, a shiver going down my spine. "It seems so *strange*."

"Unnatural?"

"It's more that I've always looked down on potions before. Now, I'm worried I won't be good enough to make one. It's all very confusing."

Owen grins. "It will be so cool if you're able to do both. Hey, if you end up being an awesome warlock too, does that mean you'll take back everything horrible you've ever said about warlocks?"

"Only on the condition that you take back everything you've ever said about witches."

"I'll consider it."

Iris suddenly pops her head up from the row in front, causing us both to jump.

"What are you guys talking about?" she asks curiously. "What's with all the whispering?"

"Uh . . . uh . . . Morgan has a thing for one of the guys on the Woodvale team," Owen blurts out. "Yeah. That's why we were whispering. She's embarrassed."

"*What?*" I say.

"WHAT?" Felix shouts, standing up on his seat a few rows away. "You have GOT to be kidding! TRAITOR! BETRAYAL TO THE MAX!"

"No, Owen is—"

"Did he ask you to the dance?" Felix rages. "Did you say yes? Huh? DID YOU?"

"No! No, Owen made the whole thing up! Excuse me for a second while I kill him for it."

Owen sniggers next to me and I elbow him sharply in the ribs. Reluctantly, I stop Merlin from crawling across to him in his spider form and giving Owen a much-deserved pinch with his fangs.

"You're dead," I hiss, before Felix launches into a tirade about how Woodvale is a school for losers and they're all going down today, prompting cheers from the rest of the coach.

I'm not feeling nervous at all about this round of the quiz. I haven't done any studying, but it doesn't matter, because I'm ready to use a little magic. I know I promised myself I wouldn't use magic again in the quiz, BUT spending time with Maverick has made me feel a lot prouder of my magical abilities.

He's promised that he will be in the audience today in a "spectacularly good disguise". Mum can't come because of work, which means I'm free to use as much magic as I like. She's promised she's going to be there for the final, so I'm not sure whether I'll get away with it then, but I'll cross that bridge when I come to it.

The coach parks on the Woodvale drive and I hop down, feeling confident. The opposing team is once again waiting to greet us with evil glares. Miss Gallagher is enthusiastic at our arrival, wearing a very pretty long-sleeved green dress and sporting a new red lipstick. Mr Hopkins looks starstruck as she welcomes him. I prepare myself for a snide comment as Sandy makes a beeline for me, but she strolls right past without a second glance.

"Owen, hi!" Sandy smiles, as he steps down from the bus behind me. "I like your jumper."

"It's just our school uniform jumper. Everyone has one," he says, surprised at the compliment.

"It looks best on you, though," she says, twirling a lock of her hair in her fingers.

"Uh . . . thanks," he says, blushing.

BLUSHING.

I immediately feel a wave of anger towards them both. What does she think she's doing? Is she trying to FLIRT with Owen? GROSS! And what is he doing, going around *blushing*?! Like a total moron! Does he think she's being SERIOUS? Does he think she means it? Can't he see right through her? WHAT IS WRONG WITH HIM?

Wait. What is wrong with me? Why am I so bothered about this?

My mind flits to what Mum said the necklace means and I shake my head, trying to shake those thoughts and feelings right out.

"Anyway," Owen croaks, gesturing to where Iris and

Kareen are huddled, "I better go join the others. Good luck ... uh ... both of you."

"Thanks! He's so sweet," Sandy sighs, watching him go. "I think I might ask him to the dance."

"WHAT?" I splutter. "As IF he would ever go with you! You're the ENEMY!"

"So immature. I think it will be nice to make some new friends. It's not all about competition, Morgan," she says, before taking my arm and moving me away from the rest of the team. "I'm glad we have a moment to talk in private. I want you to know that, this time, it will be a level playing field."

"Excuse me?"

She crosses her arms. "Did you really think I didn't know you were using magic in the last round?"

"I don't know what you're talking about."

"Oh please, you couldn't have been less subtle," she says, flicking her hair behind her shoulders. "At first I was mad about you cheating, but now I'm all for it. If you're using magic, then it's only fair if I do, too."

"Sandy, I honestly—"

"We'll see who the better witch is," she interrupts. "Once and for all."

With that, she spins around and walks away, her chin in the air. Merlin crawls out from under my shirt collar.

"This is going to be interesting," he says, not bothering to hide the glee from his voice.

"No, Merlin," I say, as any confidence I had starts to melt away. "This is going to be bad."

✦ Twenty·one ✦

Everything starts off normal.

The teams are at their tables on the opposite sides of the stage, Miss Gallagher is at the Quiz Master table in the middle, while the audience sits in excited anticipation.

Sandy and I are staring each other down, not unlike an intense duel in an old Western movie. Miss Gallagher examines her question cards to make sure they're in the right order.

"Welcome," she announces, her voice echoing around the auditorium, "to Round Three of School Challenge!"

I see Sandy's hand drop to her side, under the table. I mirror her and as the audience politely claps, I click my fingers. Sandy does the same.

It's on, Cactus-head.

The first question is called out and Felix gets there before anyone else, scoring a point for Riddle House and getting us off to a good start. Sandy mouths, "You're welcome" at me, making my blood boil. How dare she act as though she gave us a point? Felix won that fair and square.

Miss Gallagher launches into Question Two: "Hamlet is the prince of which country?"

"DENMARK!" Sandy cries as she slams the bell.

I wait for her to make eye contact with me and then I calmly mouth, "You're welcome" back at her. Her expression is thunderous.

"Who wrote *A Brief History of Time*?"

"Stephen Hawking!" I yell, ringing the bell as the words appear on my skin before sinking away again.

"What is the London address of Sherlock Holmes?"

"TWO HUNDRED AND TWENTY-ONE B BAKER STREET!" Sandy and I chorus, both pressing our bells at the same time.

Gasps and heated discussions erupt in the audience as to which of us got the answer first. We're both up on our feet as Miss Gallagher looks from one of us to the other, baffled.

"I think . . . I think that was a draw!"

Students groan and boo the boring decision, while Sandy and I slowly sit down, neither of us taking our eyes off the other. I've never felt so on edge. One moment of distraction or hesitation and Sandy will take the lead.

The scoreboard stays fairly level for the next few questions until the beginning of the next round when Sandy crosses a line, making the completely unprovoked decision to take things a step further.

We're about to launch into the first question of the sports round when Felix lets out a blood-curdling scream, leaping up on to his chair, jabbing his finger at the table.

"S-SPIDER! SPIDER!"

Holly, sitting next to him, cries out in fright as she scrambles to her feet, recoiling from the desk where a large, black, furry-legged spider is sat next to her bell, wondering what all the fuss is about.

"What the—" I whisper, standing up to examine him as the rest of the team yelps and moves away, sending the audience into fits of giggles as everyone desperately cranes their necks to see what has caused such a dramatic reaction.

"That spider was not there a moment ago," Merlin mutters in my ear.

I glance over at Sandy, who is leaning back in her seat, wearing a triumphant expression. I scoop up the poor spider, who has found himself transported from his cosy web right on to centre stage by magic. My handling of him causes Felix to let out another cry, before he starts whimpering, instructing me not to bring it anywhere near him.

Instead, I walk determinedly across the stage towards the Woodvale team and present the spider proudly in my outstretched palm. Having been rolling about with laughter at Felix's reaction, the Woodvale lot suddenly panic, jumping up and scarpering from the stage as I dart forwards at them, as though about to chase them around. Sandy is the only one who doesn't move.

The audience are thoroughly enjoying this turn of events, finding the spider incident very entertaining.

"All right, calm down, everyone, calm down!" Miss Gallagher yells above the noise, desperately attempting to bring things back to order.

A Woodvale teacher comes up to the stage and holds out her cupped hands for me.

"Here, I'll take it and put it outside," she offers, and I gratefully let the poor befuddled spider crawl over to her.

"Teams, sit down!" Miss Gallagher barks, rapping her knuckles on the table like an overzealous judge in a courtroom.

"You're not going to let her get away with that, are you?" Merlin whispers, as we all retake our seats. "Look at what she's done to your team!"

Merlin has a point. Felix looks as though he's seen a ghost, timidly taking his seat with great caution, jumping at any sign of movement in his vicinity.

When the noise has died down, Miss Gallagher resumes her questions, firing out the next one about football. Felix isn't even listening. He's too busy shuddering and wiping at his arms, thinking a spider might be on him.

The Woodvale team get the point.

"Fine," I say under my breath, glaring at Sandy as she high-fives her fellow team members, "if that's how you want to play it."

I bide my time, letting everything settle down again, allowing Miss Gallagher to continue with a few more questions. Riddle House fall behind, but thanks to the answers still appearing on my hand, I manage to bring us back level with Woodvale, despite Sandy's best efforts to beat me to the bell.

I wait for the right moment, then click my fingers. No one notices it, but a window at the back of the auditorium opens.

Miss Gallagher is about to launch into the next

question when she's interrupted by a strange *SQUAWK!* echoing off the walls. Eyes fly up to the ceiling as a large crow comes soaring through the room, swooping down over the heads of the audience members and heading straight for the Woodvale team. They screech and duck beneath the table as the crow reaches them. It circles the stage before dive-bombing them again just as they pop their heads up to see if it's gone.

I burst out laughing at their expressions, as do the Riddle House team and much of the audience. Sandy's jaw is clenched, unflinching, as the crow's wings flap past her face. Not wanting to bore the crow any longer, I release the magic so that he can fly back out again happily, having done a very good job of giving the Woodvale team a fright.

The auditorium is once again in uproar, hardly daring to believe what's just happened. I purposefully avoid catching Owen's eye, wherever he's sat among them. I know he'll be giving me that disapproving look that he has down to an art. I wonder if Maverick is in here somewhere; if he is, he'll know what's going on.

I hope he's proud of me.

"I don't know WHAT is going on today," Miss Gallagher says, flustered. "But the animal kingdom seems to be a lot livelier than normal."

I assume that Sandy agrees we are both now even when it comes to putting off other team members, and we can go back to only using magic to give us a nudge towards some answers.

But I underestimated her.

Once the auditorium has calmed and Riddle House is back on equal points to Woodvale, I hear the familiar sound of fingers clicking. And, moments later, I hear the soft fluttering of wings in the distance.

"Uh-oh," I whisper, alarmed at what is about to happen. "I know that sound. Poor Felix."

Suddenly, a swarm of bats descends upon the stage.

If anyone saw a swarm of bats flying at them, they might be a little shocked and potentially frightened, but for Felix, it's a particularly unwelcome sight after the events of last term.

Mum managed to use warlock potion to wipe his memory so that he wouldn't remember the bats that remained outside his house for ages, forcing him and his family to take refuge inside for days, but I never bothered to wipe the memory of when I got bats to chase him around the school after he said something mean to me. I'd have had to wipe the memory of everyone else in the canteen who witnessed the spectacle, not to mention those who saw it on YouTube.

"THEY'RE BACK!" he screeches at the top of his lungs.

He throws himself under the table for cover, as does the rest of the team. I expect the audience members to bolt through the doors but, as the bats remain on the stage, they all jump to their feet and gawp helplessly, not knowing what to do next.

"Don't just use your magic to attack!" Merlin points out urgently, as I wave the bats out of my face. "Defend your team!"

"Good point!"

I try to focus, ignoring the wings hitting me in the face, and I click my fingers. The spell works. The bats instantly change their mind and fly away, out of the auditorium and into the distance.

"THAT IS IT!" Miss Gallagher announces, looking completely frazzled. "This round must finish! The points are level! We shall call it a draw! We all need to get out of here! Everyone out of the auditorium! NOW!"

Her stern words have the desired effect. Everyone rushes towards the exits. I follow my team off the stage, Felix a shivering mess, glancing over his shoulder every few seconds. Holly puts an arm round him and guides him through the wings and down the corridors towards the main school exit, assuring him that the bats are gone and there definitely isn't one caught in his hair like last time.

"Morgan!"

I stop at the sound of my name, looking round at the crowd pouring from the auditorium. I don't recognize the voice.

"Morgan," the voice says again, and I turn to see an old man with a monocle and a whiskery grey beard, wearing a smart three-piece grey suit.

The bright-purple-and-yellow floral pocket square gives it away.

"Maverick?" I whisper, peering into his eyes.

He chuckles, winking at me as we sidle to the wall of the corridor, out of people's way. "Not a bad disguise, eh?"

"So cool! You don't look anything like you! How did you do it?"

"A very simple potion, if you can get your hands on the right ingredients. Perhaps I'll teach you it one day. Have you had any luck with the book?"

"Uh ... not yet," I say, slightly taken aback at his asking me these kinds of questions now. "I haven't had the chance to try anything. What did you think of the quiz?"

"Very entertaining spells."

"It may have got a *little* out of hand. Did you enjoy—"

"You could tell your magic was much stronger than

hers," he interrupts with a grin. "She's like any witch your age, but you have something special, I'm sure of it."

"Really?"

He nods. "Absolutely. I'm proud of you."

I brighten at his words. I can't believe it! He's *proud* of me!

"I can't wait to watch you in the final," he says enthusiastically. "You'll be even better!"

"You're going to come to the final? Promise?"

"I wouldn't miss it!" He laughs, rubbing his hands together. "It's an excellent opportunity to try out a few potions, if you can make them by then. I have a feeling you will. We're on to something, Morgan, I can feel it in my bones. A witch making potions. Unheard of!"

"Oh, well, I'm not sure I'll use potions or anything in the final," I say, glancing at the people still filing out of the hall and keeping my voice down. "The magic wasn't exactly subtle and if people were to get suspicious, I'm not sure it would—"

"There you go, still worrying about what people think." He chuckles, as though I've said something naïve. "That was superb magic today and extremely fun to watch, but warlock magic could be *even more* imaginative and entertaining. I have plenty I could teach you for the next round."

Sandy suddenly appears from behind Maverick. I freeze as she saunters by with an appalled expression. Dread washes over me, making my blood run cold.

She heard everything.

CHAPTER

✦ Twenty·two ✦

Maverick doesn't think it's a big deal.

He can't work out why I'm panicking. As soon as Sandy passed us, I grabbed Maverick's arm and pulled him into an empty classroom, shutting the door behind me and FREAKING OUT.

"I don't think it's so bad if she overheard," he says, as I begin to pace around the room.

"How can you not see it as a bad thing?" I ask him, exasperated.

Merlin is in his black cat form, perched on a chair, watching me go back and forth.

"What's the worst that can happen?" Maverick asks, earning a hiss from Merlin.

"She's going to tell her mum that there was a warlock

at the quiz and that she overheard him speaking to me! Then her mum will tell all the witches in our coven and my mum will have to tell everyone why and then she'll lose her position of Great Sorceress." I chew on my thumbnail nervously. "I am in SO much trouble."

"I thought we were in agreement that the rules were ridiculous," Maverick says, taking the teacher's seat at the front of the classroom and putting his feet up on the desk. It's strange talking to him in his disguise. It feels like I'm chatting to a stranger. "And anyway, I'm sure your mum can handle any of that nonsense. They have no idea who I am. Your mum can make something up."

"It doesn't matter what she makes up," I explain, irritated that he doesn't seem to be taking this situation seriously. "The point is that I shouldn't be in contact with a warlock at ALL."

"Morgan, they're all going to find out sooner or later when you dazzle the world with your potions," he says, taking a packet of sweets out of his pocket and throwing one up into the air and catching it in his mouth. He chews happily. "The witch community will be so in awe of you, they won't care about any of this."

"What about Mum?"

He shrugs. "As I've said, I'm sure she can handle

anything that comes her way. She wasn't voted in as Great Sorceress for nothing. She'll work it out."

Merlin and I share a look. I decide that Maverick isn't the best person to talk to about this. He's in his own world where rules don't apply, and as lovely as that must be, it's not really that helpful. I know Mum and I haven't exactly been seeing eye to eye recently, but I don't want her to get in trouble. It doesn't seem fair.

"I should go," I tell Maverick, getting my phone out. "I need to meet some friends. Thanks so much for coming. I appreciate the support for the quiz and everything."

"I had fun," he says, jumping up with a smile on his face. He looks pleased to have been excused from this serious conversation. "Let me know when you've had a chance to look at the book."

"I will," I tell him.

He comes over and puts a hand on my shoulder. "It's very important that you do. This school stuff isn't for ever. But your magical abilities, they're your future. So make it a priority."

"Right."

He smiles warmly at me, before giving me a wave and leaving the classroom, whistling as he saunters down the corridor to the exit. I'm typing frantically into my phone when Owen peers round the door.

"Hey!" I exclaim, putting my phone down and gesturing for him to come in and shut the door. "I was texting you!"

"I promise I wasn't snooping," he says quickly. "I saw you duck in here a minute ago with that person – who I assume is Maverick in a disguise? – and you looked stressed. I thought I might hang around and make sure everything was OK."

"It's not," I say, sitting down and burying my head in my hands as Merlin changes into a tarantula and crawls up my arm. "Sandy overheard Maverick and I talking, and he said something about being a warlock."

His eyes widen. "You're sure she overheard?"

"Yes."

"Right." He hesitates. "This isn't good."

"I know."

"Maybe she won't tell anyone," he says thoughtfully.

"Why would she keep something that huge to herself?" I ask him, biting my lip. "Ever since I turned her into a cactus, she's been waiting for an excuse to get revenge. What could be more perfect than this? She's going to get Mum fired."

"You need to tell your mum about this."

"I can't. I'm not talking to her."

"This seems like a good reason to start talking to

her again," Owen points out. "Maybe she can speak to Sandy's mum and stop the rumours before they start."

"Or there is another way to do that," I say, grimacing at the idea. "I could talk to Sandy."

Owen raises an eyebrow. "Are you serious?"

"If I can persuade her to keep it a secret, then we can keep it between us. No one else needs to know. Mum's position will be safe." I let out a sigh, throwing my head back and looking up at the ceiling. "As soon as Mum knows, she'll want to do the right thing and resign as Great Sorceress. She wouldn't go and talk to Sandy's mum. She would just step back of her own accord. It's much better if she doesn't know about this at all."

"Wow." Owen leans on the back of a chair. "You're going to ask Sandy Cadabra for a favour."

"I don't have any other options. Unless!" I sit up excitedly. "I could turn Sandy into a non-speaking cactus, but permanently this time. Then she wouldn't be able to tell anyone!"

"I think that's the BEST idea," Merlin cries from my shoulder. "Let's go!"

"Or, you could go with your first option and talk to her instead of ruining her life for ever," Owen says, the corners of his mouth twitching as he tries and fails to suppress a smile.

"UGH." I scowl at him. "I wish I hadn't even suggested that. The second option is a LOT more fun."

"Don't listen to the warlock," Merlin says. "Listen to your heart. Your heart is saying cactus spell. That Casper won't know what's hit him."

Owen looks confused. "Casper?"

"Sandy's familiar," I sigh.

"Look, you need to talk to Sandy to find out exactly what she overheard," Owen says firmly. "Maverick was in disguise, so she doesn't have a clue who he is. Maybe she'll keep quiet."

"HA!"

"She's not a monster, Morgan. Even though she is a witch. So, that's bad enough. Maybe you could apologize to her about the cactus thing, too," he adds, giving me an encouraging nudge with his elbow. "Two birds with one stone."

I narrow my eyes at him. "You weren't there. She *deserved* to be turned into a cactus."

"Maybe, but don't you think it's about time that you two cleared the air? And apologizing to her for that may put her in a better mood for when it comes to asking her to keep a secret for you. Don't you think?"

"Fine. I'll think about it."

Owen hesitates. "While we're on the subject of you

and Sandy. That magic you both used during the quiz today. . ."

"I know, I know, I shouldn't be using magic at school, especially after everything that went wrong last term blah blah blah," I huff. "You don't have to give me the lecture."

"I wasn't going to lecture you. I was just going to ask why you felt you needed to use magic in the first place? I know you used it for the second round, too. Why?"

"Duh! I *had* to use magic," I say, folding my arms.

He frowns in confusion. "Why?"

"I was letting down my team! We were going to lose because of me. I didn't want them to have to suffer just because I'm the weakest link."

"You were only the weakest link because everyone else had studied for it and you tried to cram it all in your brain at the last minute," he says, irritated.

"I should never have been on the quiz team in the first place. It's all your fault."

"Morgan," he says, exasperated, "did you use magic in the first round of the quiz?"

"No. But that's not—"

"And you got some of the answers. Even though you hadn't even practised that much for it, right?"

"Yeah, but that was lucky."

He shakes his head. "No, it's because you knew the

answers to the questions. That tends to happen when you research and read stuff. Look, what I'm trying to say is, you don't need magic. If you put your mind to it, I think you could do really well on this quiz team. And I do think you need to be more careful – those were strange goings-on in that hall. You should have seen the look on Iris's face. She had her eyes on you the whole time."

I gulp, hoping that I was clicking my fingers subtly. "Really?"

"Like she was studying you. I think it's important you don't use magic in the next round. You have to agree. It got strange out there and people aren't stupid."

I frown, absent-mindedly fiddling with the chain of my necklace. "Maverick thinks I should use more magic, and focus less on this school stuff."

"That doesn't seem surprising." Owen smiles. "He's *Maverick Moonshine*. His life is magic. But if you don't want your mum to get in trouble, you need to tone down the attack-bats and swooping crows."

I sit quietly for a moment. It doesn't feel good being the cause of Mum getting in trouble, whether she's upset me or not. I have to make things right.

"Are you sure it wouldn't be easier to turn Sandy into a cactus for life?" I ask Owen.

"Oh, it would definitely be easier," he says with a grin. "But what witch doesn't love a challenge?"

I press the doorbell and then quickly take two giant steps back, so I'm not too close.

Owen offered to come with me for moral support, but as it's a witch's house, he's staying well clear, hovering on the pavement a few houses away, out of sight.

The door swings open and a man stands in the doorway.

"Hello!" he says brightly, greeting me with a warm smile. "I recognize you! Aren't you on the Riddle House quiz team?"

"Yes, hi," I say timidly, giving a small wave. "I'm Morgan."

"Nice to meet you, Morgan. Wasn't that last round nuts?!" He chuckles. "Never seen anything like it. I'm glad no one was hurt. It was like a strange zoo!"

"It was strange, yeah." I clear my throat. "Is Sandy in?"

"Sure," he says, before calling her name over his shoulder and then turning back to me. "Do you want to come in?"

"Actually, I'm in a bit of a rush, so don't worry," I say, knowing that Sandy will be furious at me for being anywhere near her house, let alone strolling in and making myself comfortable.

Sandy appears behind him and he tells us he'll leave us to it, giving me a cheery wave before disappearing back inside. Sandy leans on the doorframe, folding her arms and looking me up and down.

"What are *you* doing here?" she asks suspiciously.

I take a deep breath, recalling what Owen and I discussed I would say on the way here.

"I'm here to apologize," I say, hating every word.

She looks confused.

"For two things," I continue, clearing my throat. "Firstly, for the magic getting out of control today. And secondly, for that time I turned you into a cactus."

She sniffs. When she doesn't say anything, I keep going.

"And I also came here to suggest we don't use magic in the final round."

It's a reluctant suggestion, but Owen's convinced me it's the right thing to do. I hate the idea of disappointing Maverick, but as much fun as it's been using magic, and as much as I hate the idea of how much studying I'm going to have to do, we can't risk anything like that happening again. I'm not sure I want to be responsible for destroying the secrecy which has shrouded magic folk for centuries.

I am making this EXTREMELY selfless sacrifice for the sake of the witch community.

Sandy watches me carefully and then, rolling her eyes, lets out a long sigh.

"Fine. You're right. I guess it was a bit risky." She shifts her weight from one foot to the other. "And also my mum was really angry about it."

"My mum would have been, too."

She nods. "So, we have a deal then."

"Yes. Deal."

She purses her lips. "We should talk about that old man at the quiz."

My whole body tenses. "Yeah, look—"

"How long have you known that your teacher was a warlock?" she asks icily.

I blink at her. "W-what?"

"I heard him, Morgan, so don't try to deny it. He said he still had lots to teach you. When did you find out he was a warlock?"

"Oh ... I ... not long ago! Yeah, just before that round of the quiz," I manage to say, going with it. "It was a shock. A big shock."

She makes a face. "What are you going to do? You can't stay at a school where your teacher is a warlock? I can't believe you were even talking to him."

"Actually, he's not a teacher at the school. He's ... um ... he's a tutor. A quiz tutor. And he's been fired! So I won't ever see him again."

She looks relieved on my behalf. "That's something. Trust Riddle House to be stupid enough to hire a warlock."

"Sandy, I was wondering," I begin, desperately, "I know it's a lot to ask, but would you mind keeping it a secret? I'm embarrassed that there was a warlock right under my nose and I didn't know. I was hoping we could ... forget all about it? If you've already told your mum, then maybe you could ask her not to tell anyone either. Please?"

She ponders my request, clearly relishing the moment.

"I won't tell anyone," she says eventually, with a superior expression, like a queen pardoning her subject. "And I haven't told Mum, yet."

"Really?" I check, surprised it didn't take more persuading. "You promise you won't tell?"

She nods, before looking down at the ground shamefully. "Look, last year I went to a drama camp and I didn't realize until the very end of the summer that there was a warlock there. She was even in the same improvisation class as me. I had no idea and it was *mortifying*. So, the truth is, I get it. I won't tell if you won't."

"Right. Great! I won't. I promise."

"When I found out, I turned her into a cactus," she says, smiling at the memory. "Ever since you did it to me, I've been practising that spell. It was very satisfying to see her like that."

I wince in embarrassment. "Yeah, again, I really am sorry about that."

She shrugs. "In the end, it inspired me. That warlock looked like such an idiot. A cactus in a T-shirt and trousers is very funny."

"It sounds very funny."

"Warlocks suck."

"Mmm," I reply, and I can see from her expression that she's taken that as a "yes".

"Well, would you look at that," Casper says, in orange-tabby-cat form at Sandy's feet. "They've finally agreed on something."

"Don't think this makes us friends," Merlin hisses back, as a black cat next to me. "Our witches are still enemies."

"Of course." Casper shrugs. "It wouldn't be as fun if they were friends, now, would it?"

Sandy and I share an awkward smile.

"Well then, guess I'll see you at the next quiz," she says eventually, her expression hardening. "Prepare for your team to be humiliated on television. I hope you've been working on your loser face."

"Yeah? I hope you've been working on your ... your stupid face," I retort.

She shakes her head at my lame response. "I'll see you at the final."

For some unknown reason, I give her a weird salute, and then turn on my heel and march away, with Merlin now in his tarantula form on my shoulder. We hear the door shut behind us and I breathe a sigh of relief.

"Well?" Owen asks when we get to him. "Did she accept your apology?"

"She did."

"And what about Maverick?"

"It's all fine. She's not going to tell. She thinks he's a Riddle House tutor who's now been fired, so we're all good."

"All's well that ends well," he says cheerily as we walk towards the bus stop. "So, you and Sandy are friends, then?"

"No way," I say, wrinkling my nose. "But I can respect her as an adversary."

He sighs. "You are sounding more and more like Merlin every day."

"She wishes," Merlin says snootily. "So, what are we doing now?"

"We're going home to study for the final," I say determinedly. "Owen, are you busy right now?"

"Nope. Why?"

"How do you feel about a study group?" I ask, smiling at him hopefully. "If I can't use magic for this quiz, I'm going to need all the help I can get."

CHAPTER

✦ Twenty·three ✦

The next time I see Maverick is two weeks later, a few days before the final round of the quiz. He's cancelled twice on his planned visits recently, because he's been working on a new potion that gives you the ability to read another person's thoughts and apparently he had a major breakthrough. He's been working on this potion for years, he told me, so he couldn't risk taking a break in case his thought process was interrupted and he forgot the potential key to the whole thing.

He rang this morning to say he could meet me after school. It was a little last minute, but that doesn't matter to me. I'm excited to see him.

So far today, Mum's managed to stop herself from saying anything about how he expects the world to revolve around him and drop anything to fit in with his schedule, comments that she's made a few times since Maverick reappeared in our lives. Since our fight, though, she's been tiptoeing around me.

I still haven't really forgiven Mum from losing it over the necklace and banning me from being Owen's friend, but I have to admit that I miss her. Our house is always silent at the moment, because we're not talking or hanging out, and I've been getting the bus to and from school so I don't have to be stuck in a car with her.

I know she feels bad about the fight. She gets this sad look in her eye whenever I get up to leave the table straight after dinner so I can hide away in my room. The other day, I was brushing my teeth and she came to stand in the doorway of the bathroom. I paused mid-brushing, wondering what she wanted.

"I hope that Owen has been understanding," she'd said carefully, wearing a sad expression. "I do know that it's hard to end a friendship and put a stop to . . . feelings. You know that I've been there; I know how that feels. But it will get easier as time goes on, and I want you to know. . ." She'd paused here to take a deep breath. "Well, I want you to know that you can always talk to me about it, or, if you want a good cry with me there, you can do that, too."

I'd stared at her, toothpaste dribbling down my chin.

"I'm fine," I'd said eventually, before turning back to the mirror and continuing to brush my teeth.

She'd nodded and then wandered off, leaving me to it. I feel bad about that exchange because my reaction was so cold. But the reason I don't need to go to her and be all sad about ending my friendship with Owen is because I haven't actually done it.

I try hard not to think about what she told me about the necklace. When I do I get this weird mix of feelings, excitement and nerves all at the same time. Part of me, the main part, hopes that the necklace is VERY dramatic and has turned black purely because I'm friends with a warlock.

But there's also a tiny part, TEENY tiny, that wonders if maybe the necklace isn't so wrong.

When I think about it, Owen and I do spend a lot of time together. Yeah, he can be super annoying and all superior about warlocks. But I also really enjoy his company and he does make me laugh a lot and I guess I care about his opinion. He always makes sure I'm included at school and he has always helped me when I've got into trouble, which he doesn't *have* to do.

And I do kind of get fluttery butterflies in my stomach when he smiles at me.

But none of that means anything. I don't think.

"Are you looking forward to seeing your dad today?" Mum suddenly asks, jolting me from my thoughts about Owen. When I'd told her that Maverick wanted to see me after school today, she'd asked if she could drive me to meet him from school. I'd said that she didn't need to because I could get the bus, but she'd insisted.

I realize I've lifted my hand to rest over my pendant where it's sitting under my shirt and quickly drop it down to my lap again. I hope Mum didn't notice. Luckily she's driving, so has her eyes firmly forward.

"Yeah, I'm excited to see him," I answer breezily, giving Merlin, who is in his rat form on my lap, a tickle under the chin. "He wants to tell me all about this new potion he's working on. It would let warlocks read minds."

Mum raises her eyebrows. "I remember him working on that one years ago. I'm surprised he's still trying. He was warned off it."

"What do you mean?"

"Do you think it would be a good thing for warlocks to have the power to read people's minds?" she asks simply. "Would you like it if someone could read yours?"

My face grows hot at the thought. Mum would find out that I'm still friends with Owen. And Owen would find out about the necklace and what it means.

"No!" I yell, a little more forcefully than necessary. I clear my throat and say breezily, "I mean, probably not."

"A potion like that would be very handy when it comes to taking over the world," Merlin points out gleefully. "Think of the secrets you could discover!"

"It would be very invasive," Mum says, ignoring him. "The Chief Warlock told Maverick to give up on it a long time ago, outlining how dangerous it would be, but it would seem that hasn't put him off."

She pulls into the parking area next to the woods and turns off the engine. We're a little early as I'd factored in waiting for the bus when I agreed a time with Maverick. As I unclip my seatbelt, she reaches to her bag in the backseat and pulls out a little box with a ribbon around it. She holds it out for me.

"What is this?" I ask, swivelling in my seat to face her.

"I've seen how hard you've been working towards the quiz the last couple of weeks and I thought this might come in useful," she explains. "Open it."

I take the box and undo the ribbon. Lifting the lid, I see a shiny silver bell sitting on tissue paper, the same type of bell we've been using in the quiz rounds.

"It's so you can practise hitting the bell quickly, as well as answering the questions," she says hurriedly, in case I don't get it.

"Mum, this is amazing." I look up at her and smile. "Thank you."

"You're welcome," she says, smiling back. "I know how important the quiz is to you. I hope this comes in handy. I can't wait for the final. Whatever happens, I'm proud of all the work you've been putting in."

"Thanks, Mum."

She nods and then sighs, glancing out of the window. Maverick has appeared and he's tapping his watch impatiently.

"Your dad is here. You should go."

I close the lid of the box and put it carefully into my backpack. "Thanks again, Mum. I'll see you later."

"See you later," she says, trying not to look too down as I shut the door and hurry off to join Maverick.

"We don't have much time," he says as I approach him, gesturing for me to lead the way down the path. "I need to get back to my study. I need to look over a few more ingredients."

"OK," I say, picking up the pace. "Thanks for coming to see me even when you're busy."

"There isn't any chance that cow hair might be of use," he mumbles to himself, so deep in thought he hasn't heard me. "No, I tried that one. Perhaps sap squeezed from daffodil stems? Or the leg of a dead beetle? Maybe a dash of pond algae. Yes, algae might make sense. I should write that down."

"What do you want to do today?" I ask as we reach the clearing, hoping that none of the potions he's given me have included beetle legs or algae.

He has stopped at the edge and is writing something in his notebook. I wait for him to put the notebook away and then he claps his hands.

"Right," he says, stepping towards me, "sorry about that. Need to write ideas down when they come to me or I might lose them, you see. Have you brought the book?"

I blink at him. "What book?"

"My book!" he says, putting his hands on his hips. "How else are we going to create potions?"

"I didn't bring the book," I admit, feeling bad. "Sorry, I didn't realize that I was supposed to."

"Ah. Well, no matter," he says, disappointed. "Instead, you can tell me how you're getting on. Which potions have you liked best and, more importantly, which ones have you tried? Very nice of that Irwin boy to lend you his beginner's cauldron, but I'll make sure I send you a better one."

"Owen," I correct, taking my backpack off. "I haven't got round to looking at the book yet."

He gives me a strange look, his forehead furrowed.

"But I thought we discussed this being a priority."

"It is," I say hurriedly, "but I've had a lot of studying to do for the quiz on top of homework. I haven't had much time."

"You don't need to study for the quiz, Morgan," he says grumpily. "You have magic for that."

"Actually, Sandy and I made a pact not to use magic for the final round. We both felt it would be too risky. That's why I've been working so hard. I don't want to let my team down."

"So, you're telling me that over the last few weeks you've done nothing about the potions."

I can't bear his disappointed tone. He's acting as though I've let him down, as though I haven't lived up to his expectations. I'm desperate to make it up to him somehow.

"The final of the quiz is next week and then I promise I'll put all my energy into reading your book and finding out if I can do potions."

"Yes, but I'm here now," he says, irritated, reaching for his notebook again. "I'm not sure when I'll next be able to get to you. I've got a lot of work on. I was very much hoping to see what you could do. The sooner you start, the better. We can't tell the world until you've created a successful magical potion, and it would be good to get the news out there before the summer. Then we could do a summer tour."

"What tour?" asks Merlin, sitting on my shoulder in monkey form.

"Yeah, what tour?" I repeat.

"A tour of magical potion demonstrations," Maverick explains, jotting something down. "We'll start with the UK and then go global."

"Wait, what? What are you talking about? I don't want to do a tour."

Maverick looks up from his notebook. "A tour would be absolutely necessary. Otherwise how else will we prove what you can do?"

"Why would we need to prove what I can do?"

"Morgan," he says, tilting his head at me, "I don't think you realize how *unique* you are. Witches and warlocks will be fascinated by you. You'll be a star! You will have the power to change the world."

"Whoa," I say, holding up my hands and feeling suddenly breathless. "I don't want all that. I don't want to be a star. I just want to get through school."

"School?" Maverick wrinkles his nose in disgust. "Why are you so fixated on all this school nonsense? Think about what's important! Think of the magical discoveries you have ahead of you; the test of your abilities and limitations. You can't learn any of that in school. That's why I'm so surprised you have neglected your magical ambitions in favour of some little quiz that you could easily win with the click of your fingers."

"I'm not sure I have that many magical ambitions," I say carefully. "I want to be able to create potions. I would love to try to see if I can. But I don't want to do tours and stuff like that. I'm not exactly great under pressure and this whole *star* thing, it sounds like a lot of pressure."

Maverick stares at me, baffled. "I see. That's a shame."

He looks down at the ground in deep thought for a few moments, before lifting his head and opening his mouth to say something. He thinks better of it, though, snaps his mouth shut and bows his head, once again in deep thought.

I feel terrible. I want to tell him that I'm not ungrateful and I'm not taking my magical abilities for granted, but I don't have the chance because suddenly, his eyes light up and he clicks his fingers with an enthusiastic "Aha!"

He reaches for his notebook and pen and begins to scribble frantically, muttering under his breath as he goes. Merlin and I wait patiently for him to finish, but he takes his time, crouching down on a log on the opposite side of the clearing, so that he can write in his book easier, almost as though he's forgotten we're there.

I decide to be helpful – and I guess, I'm trying to make things up to him – and click my fingers. A comfortable office chair appears, along with a desk and a lamp.

"Excellent, thank you!" he says, flashing me a smile, before he pulls himself up to the desk. "I won't be a moment."

After a couple of minutes, I click my fingers to create my own chair and Merlin transforms into a black cat, curling up on my lap for a snooze.

"Just as I thought," Maverick eventually says, looking over to me. "I'm going to need a specific ancient spell book."

"If you want we could go to Blaze Books," I suggest, pleased I might be able to help in some way. "They have some ancient sorcery books in there. You know my friend Owen, it's his—"

"No, no, no," Maverick says, shaking his head. "This is not the sort of book you can find in bookshops. There's only one known copy in existence and it disappeared years ago. There are rumours, however, that it is part of a private collection in Nepal. I'll have to go see for myself."

"You mean, go to Nepal?"

He looks over at me in the chair, Merlin asleep on my lap, and then claps his hands together, jumping to his feet and closing his notebook, tucking it safely away in his pocket.

"I'm sorry, Morgan, you're waiting for an adventure and here I am, wasting our time together by working!"

"That's OK! Your work is very important. And I wasn't waiting for an adventure," I say, wincing as Merlin stands up and stretches, digging his sharp claws into my legs. "I was waiting for you. We can sit and talk if you want. That way, if you have a brainwave or anything, you can get it written down quickly."

"Nonsense," he says with a wave of his hand, before revealing a bunch of new vials in the other. "You know me, Morgan. There are always more adventures to be had!"

"You won't be going to Nepal soon, will you?" I ask in a casual voice, selecting one of the potions on offer.

"I hope so!"

"But you'll be back in time for the final round of the quiz?" I say hopefully.

"Oh yes! When is that again?"

"Next Friday," I remind him, smiling because I've told him several times already. "It starts at two p.m. and it's at Riddle House. You'll have to come in a new disguise, so that Sandy doesn't get suspicious. She thinks the old man you came as last time is a teacher, who has now been fired."

"Lovely."

"Afterwards we have a big school dance with

Woodvale. It should be quite fun. Although, I haven't actually thought about what I'm going to wear yet."

That piques his interest. "Something spectacular, I hope?"

I laugh. "I have no idea. I'm not very good at that sort of thing."

"Your style expresses who you are," he says, gesturing to the high-collared red coat he has on today.

"I've never been very good at that," I admit.

He smiles at me, and then takes the vial I've picked to remove the cork. But I want to check something before we go on whatever adventure we're about to step into.

"Maverick," I begin, taking the potion from him and swilling it around the bottle, "you're not angry, are you? About the summer tour and things."

"Angry? No, of course not," he says, brushing a leaf off his coat. "You can't force someone to be someone they're not." He hesitates, before giving me a grin. "Unless you have the right kind of potion, that is."

I give a weak laugh and we continue with our normal routine. He instructs me on how many gulps to take, he does the same, and then we step into another world. But something is different. Something doesn't feel quite right. I tell myself that Maverick is distracted by his work, that's all.

Nothing for me to worry about.

✦ Twenty·four ✦

I slump down on my bed and bury my head in my hands.

"I DON'T KNOW WHAT TO WEAR!" I cry out.

Hanging from my curtain rail in his bat form, Merlin lets out a pointed sigh.

"Teenagers! You're so dramatic. Just pick something! Anything!"

"You're not exactly helping, Merlin," I growl, looking up at him. "You've made a rude comment about everything I've tried on."

"You say rude, I say honest."

"What am I going to do?" I huff, lying back across my bed and staring up at the ceiling. "The dance is TOMORROW."

It has been a stressful afternoon. Luckily, we have

to wear our school uniform for the quiz final tomorrow, so at least I don't have to think about what to wear on TV. But the problem is, I still haven't found an outfit for the dance.

When you're a witch, shopping is made that little bit easier. You click your fingers and, in a flash, you're wearing whatever you want. The trouble is that I *don't know* what I want and I don't seem to be getting any closer to working it out.

The school has given everyone the afternoon off in preparation for all the excitement tomorrow. While the rest of my class have either gone shopping together for last-minute accessories for the dance or are outside enjoying the afternoon sunshine, I've been holed up in my room since lunchtime going through practice questions, feeling sick with nerves. I don't really have the patience or the time to be struggling with this outfit decision.

I keep hearing Maverick's voice in my head, reminding me that fashion is about expressing yourself, showing who you are. I seem to be stuck on that bit.

I tried a lilac gown with an interesting collar, but it was too old-fashioned. "Perfect," Merlin had said about that one, "for a dance in the nineteen fifties."

And so then I clicked my fingers and was wearing a pink minidress. "Too try-hard," he'd commented as I examined it. "Wear it if you want people like Felix to point and laugh at you."

I clicked my fingers and suddenly had on a long, fitted navy dress. "That's a dress for an elegant and sophisticated young woman," he'd said. "It doesn't suit you at all."

Next I tried a spaghetti-strap red dress with a chiffon skirt. "No, no, no," was the feedback.

Then a yellow skater dress. "You look like Big Bird," Merlin had yawned. "Great, if that's the look you're going for?"

Finally, I clicked my fingers and summoned my current outfit, a pinstriped three-piece suit. "Very cool," Merlin had said. "You WISH you could pull that off."

The most annoying thing is, Merlin's been right about all of them. None seem to look quite right on me. As I roll on to my front and scream in frustration into my pillow, there's a knock on my bedroom door.

Mum appears, carrying a large box, with Helena by her feet in her elegant Bengal cat form.

"How is it going in here?" she asks tentatively.

"Badly," I say, my voice muffled by the pillow.

"Morgan has very little sense of style," Merlin comments, swooping down to the bed and transforming into a hyena, giving himself a good scratch behind the ear. "She is more of a sheep than a shepherd when it comes to fashion, if you know what I mean."

"She has a very good style," Helena retorts, sitting on my bedroom floor and narrowing her eyes at Merlin. "It's unique."

"I'm going to agree with Merlin on this one," I admit, sitting up. "I have no idea what I'm going to wear to this dance! Why wasn't I more organized? Everyone else has had their outfit planned for weeks."

"You've had a lot going on," Mum says gently, coming to perch on the edge of the bed, resting the box on her lap. "How are you feeling about tomorrow?"

"Nervous. I've been practising a lot, though." I hesitate, looking up at her. "Thanks again for the bell, Mum, it's been really helpful."

"I'm glad. Dora and I are so excited to be in the audience tomorrow, cheering you on. No matter what happens, I'm very proud of you."

"Thanks, Mum," I say, giving her a warm smile.

"I mean it. It takes a lot of guts to be a part of something like this. I feel like you've come a long way since the beginning of term."

"Yeah, well, I hated being on the quiz team at first, but it hasn't been all bad. People at school seem to like me a bit more because of it, so that's good."

It's not just Felix who seems less repulsed by me than normal; some of my other classmates have definitely started to include me in conversations more and laugh at me less during P.E. lessons. Zoey and Lucy asked my opinion on their outfits for the dance and Kareen gave Felix and I first choice of the brownies she baked the other day because we were, in her words, "quiz heroes".

The best thing about this change is that I know I'm not going to do anything to mess it up this time. Last term, my popularity was down to magic and it evaporated as soon as the magic stopped. That's not going to happen this term. Tomorrow I'm going out on stage as myself, without any magical help. I'm not going to be backing out of anything or letting anyone down last minute.

The only person who doesn't seem to be consumed by either the quiz or the dance is Iris. She's been so busy after school, no one has really seen her much. I assumed it was because she was focusing on the dance team, but Holly mentioned the other day that they haven't had many practices recently as the next dance contest isn't until after the holidays. I've caught her looking at me strangely a few times, too, and when I told Owen my suspicions he got this funny look on his face and said that she'd visited his bookshop that week, asking

280

Owen's dad if he stocked any books on magical myths and legends.

"That doesn't sound good," I'd said to Owen, horrified. "It sounds like she may be on to something."

"Yeah, and you know Iris. If she puts her mind to it, she can do anything," he'd pointed out. "She can't really be convincing herself that magic is real, though, right? Maybe we're being paranoid."

"It's hard to tell. What should we do?"

"What can we do? We have to wait and see," he'd said, glancing across the school yard to where Iris was sat on a bench reading a book.

She'd looked up at that very moment and stared at us. We'd both looked away quickly.

But I can't worry about any of that right now. I have to stay focused on the quiz AND work out what I'm going to wear to the dance. I'm running out of time.

"This arrived for you," Mum says, tapping the lid of the box with her manicured fingernail.

"What is it?"

She reaches into her pocket and pulls out a letter, placing it carefully on top of the box. "This came with it."

The letter looks familiar. It is written on old magical parchment. I place the box on the bed and open the letter. Merlin comes to read it over my shoulder.

Dear Morgan,

I am sorry to tell you that I will not be able to make it to watch you in the final of the quiz. Nepal couldn't wait. I hope you understand.

Please accept this gift, which I hope will go some way in making things up to you. I hope our paths will cross again soon.

Until then, remember, life is what you make it.

Make it magic.

Maverick

I pass the letter to Mum so she can read it, my heart sinking, my eyes prickling with hot tears. I don't want to cry. I tell myself it's stupid to cry over this. He's Maverick Moonshine. I should be proud that he's busy doing very important things for the magical community. He doesn't have time for silly school stuff. He said so himself.

"Morgan," Mum says gently, putting the letter down, "I'm so sorry."

"It's fine," I say, trying to convince myself at the same time. "He ... he told me about Nepal. I shouldn't be surprised. It's more important than a stupid quiz. It doesn't matter."

Mum doesn't say anything as I pull the box towards

me and open the lid. Inside is a beautiful, long black dress with intricately-laced sleeves. On top of the dress, a note in Maverick's handwriting says, *Thought this would suit you. Enjoy the dance.*

I stare at the note for a moment and then pull out the dress, standing up and holding it against me to check my reflection in the mirror.

"What do you think?" Mum asks.

"I think it's perfect," I reply, unable to keep the sadness out of my voice.

I click my fingers and a hanger appears for the dress, lifting it from my hands and sliding it neatly into my wardrobe. Mum watches me carefully.

"Are you all right, Morgan? If you want to talk about it—"

"I'm fine, honestly. But I should get on with practising for the quiz, so. . ."

I trail off, gesturing to the question cards scattered across my desk. Mum nods and gets up to leave, pausing in the doorway.

"If you need anything, I'm right here," she says.

"I know." I muster a smile. "But I'm really OK."

She looks unconvinced, but she gets the message and leaves the room with Helena, shutting the door behind them. I appreciate her offer, I really do, and I'm happy that we're starting to be ourselves again around each other. But I can't talk about Maverick stuff to her.

There's only one person I feel I can talk to, about it all.

CHAPTER

+Twenty-five+

Owen answers on the second ring.

"Morgan, I'm so sorry," he says down the phone, after I've filled him in on Maverick's letter. "Are you OK?"

"I feel stupid for being down about it. I've only known him a few weeks."

"Yeah, but he's your dad," Owen says simply.

"Do you think he'll ever come back?" I ask, staring at Maverick's letter. "He hasn't said an exact time. Just about our paths crossing again."

"He will come back," Owen assures me.

"But what if he only got back in touch because he was expecting me to aim to be a big star like he wanted? When I last saw him, it was different. He was angry at me for not putting magic first, for caring about anything else. He wanted me to change the world. I wasn't who he thought I was. I didn't have his ambition. I think. . ." I pause here, a lump in my throat, desperate not to let my voice crack. "I think I let him down."

"I don't believe that," Owen says firmly. "And if that is true, then he doesn't deserve you for a daughter. Some things are more important than magic."

I smile into the phone. "Yeah. I guess I just wish Maverick thought that, too. Anyway – " I wipe a tear from my cheek and take a deep breath – "who cares? That's what *he* would say, right? I should do my own thing; stop caring about what anyone else thinks. I've got to stay positive and focused on tomorrow."

"How are you feeling about tomorrow night?" Owen asks. "Are you excited?"

"Not exactly. But I've done all the preparation I can," I say, slumping back into my pillows. "I'll keep running through practice questions."

"I meant the dance." Owen laughs.

"Oh. Yeah, I don't think I'll go to that."

"*What?*" He sounds surprised. "Why not?"

"Because my dad just ditched me. I don't really feel like dancing right now."

There's silence down the line and I feel bad for being so snappy.

"It's only a dance," I add hurriedly, trying to sound a bit more upbeat. "I'll go to the next one. And I'll probably be tired after the quiz. I'll want to come home and wallow. It will be nice to spend some time with Mum." I suddenly feel as though I might start crying again. "Anyway, I should go. Got lots of stuff to do. Sorry for ranting. I'll see you tomorrow, Owen."

I hang up before he can say anything.

I try to rally myself to get some work done, but I'm feeling too down to concentrate. I'm such an idiot. Mum was right about Maverick all along. I really believed that he might put me before his next adventure. But the magic is too important to him. I lie down on my bed, letting the tears flow, staring up at the ceiling. I should have done what he said. I should have tried making a potion. Then he wouldn't have gone away.

"He would have gone away no matter what," Merlin says suddenly, coming to sit on my stomach as a black cat. "It's nothing to do with you."

"Doesn't feel that way," I say, but it's nice of him to have tried to comfort me, so I reach out and stroke his head.

The doorbell rings and I hear Mum's footsteps going down the stairs, before the door opens and the sound of muffled voices follows. I assume it's Dora, coming over to wish me luck for tomorrow, but it's not a woman's voice.

"Morgan!" Mum's voice calls up the stairs. "You have a visitor."

I push myself up off the bed and try not to get my hopes up. Maverick would not have sent that letter unless he meant it. Maybe it's Howard and Puffin, wondering if I'd like to join them for a walk or something.

I traipse down the stairs with Merlin. We freeze on the bottom step when we see who it is.

"Hi," Owen says, smiling up at me.

Mum is standing VERY tensely. I'm amazed she hasn't slammed the door in his face or yelled at him. Instead of doing either of those things, she takes a deep breath and clears her throat.

"I shall leave you to it," she announces, before gliding away into the sitting room.

I watch her go, baffled, before turning back to Owen.

"What are you doing here? My mum—"

"I'm not scared of her," he says breezily, as though it's no big deal he's shown up to the house of the Great Sorceress, who is supposed to be his greatest enemy and has the power to ruin his life.

"You're going to be in so much trouble!"

"Like I just told your mum, I don't care," he tells me. "I wanted to make sure you're OK."

I feel so overwhelmed that I'm scared I might start crying again. All these tears are so unlike me. But now they've started, they won't seem to stop.

"You hung up the phone before I could say everything," he continues. "I wanted to tell you that even if Maverick isn't there to support you tomorrow, I will be. And so will your mum and Dora, and Iris and all our class. Everyone is going to be cheering for you, and Maverick is missing out."

"Thanks, Owen," I manage to say, more grateful than he imagines. "I can't believe you risked coming here to tell me that."

"That wasn't why I risked coming here."

He looks down at his shoes anxiously and then lifts his eyes to meet mine before he speaks again.

"The reason I came here is to ask you to the dance."

I blink at him. "W-what?"

"You can't let Maverick ruin tomorrow for you. I won't let you. You've worked hard and you deserve some fun," he says hurriedly, tripping over his words. "So, I don't want you to not go to the dance. I think you should go. And I want you to go with me. Will you?"

"Go with you, as in . . . your date?" I say, hardly daring to believe it.

"Yeah." He grins at me, relaxing a little. "As in my date."

I hear movement behind me and swivel round to see Mum standing in the hall, watching us. She's clearly been listening to the whole conversation. My heart sinks as she comes over, preparing for her to angrily remind Owen that we're forbidden from being friends. Owen lifts his chin up defiantly as she approaches him. We both know what's coming.

"I think," she begins, "that you two going to the dance together sounds like a lot of fun."

Owen's eyes widen in surprise. My jaw drops open. Merlin gasps.

"S-*seriously?*" Owen stutters, thrown.

"Seriously," she replies firmly, looking him up and down. "I have a feeling I wouldn't be able to stop you anyway. Warlocks are notoriously stubborn." She pauses, her voice softening. "But who knew they could be so brave?"

She turns her attention to me as Owen's cheeks flush pink – he's astonished by the unexpected compliment.

"Sorry for interrupting," she says drily to me. "I thought I should let you know my thoughts just in case. I'll let you give your answer now."

With that, she marches away down the hall and into

the kitchen, making herself scarce. I turn back to Owen, who is smiling broadly.

"I wasn't expecting her to say that." He laughs.

"Me neither," I say, stunned.

"So," he prompts nervously, frowning as he tries to read my expression, "do you want to go to the dance with me?"

"Yeah," I say, the butterflies somersaulting in joy around my stomach, "I'd love to."

CHAPTER

✦ Twenty·six ✦

The atmosphere in the Green Room is very intense.

We've all been introduced to the TV crew who are filming the final, including a slick-haired up-and-coming local presenter, Fred, who is stepping into the role of Quiz Master. Mr Hopkins was a little put out but then Miss Gallagher suggested they sit together in the audience and he didn't seem to mind being replaced any more.

We've been told that someone will come get us when we have to take our places on stage, and since then, everyone has been more or less silent. Felix is chewing his thumbnail nervously; Holly is pacing by the window, running through facts under her breath; Jacob is sitting at a desk studying last-minute notes; and Ivy is trying to distract herself by scrolling through social media, pretending nothing out of the ordinary is about to happen.

Sandy and the Woodvale team look equally on edge on the other side of the room. I've noticed that Sandy has checked her pristine make-up at least five times in the last ten minutes. I tried to put a bit of lipstick on, but Merlin took one look at me and said I reminded him of my Great Aunt Hilda at her eighty-fifth birthday party, so I rubbed it right off.

The door suddenly bangs open and Mr Hopkins and Miss Gallagher appear.

"All right, teams," Miss Gallagher says with a big smile, scanning the room and making eye contact with every one of us. "It's time to go on."

"Remember," Mr Hopkins says as we get ready to file out of the room, "go out there and have fun!"

He politely lets the Woodvale team go out first, led by Miss Gallagher towards the auditorium, before he turns to us and adds quietly, "You kick their butts!"

We all giggle, grateful for a bit of light relief.

As we walk out on to the stage, there is thunderous applause. The cameras aren't rolling yet and there are all these people still setting up microphones and doing sound checks. Fred is sitting with his eyes closed, clutching the question cards at his desk, while someone else powders his nose.

"Make sure there's no shine," he's instructing anxiously.

I take my seat and scan the sea of faces in the audience. It's nice to see some of the students have made banners saying things like, "Go Riddle House!" but I gasp when I notice the best sign of all, a huge colourful and glittery banner reading, "MORGAN RULES!" Dora's face appears from behind it and she gives me a big thumbs-up as she sees me noticing it. I spot Mum sitting next to her, trying not to get hit in the face, dodging the banner every time Dora waves it about enthusiastically.

I share a smile with Mum. I'm pleased she's here.

"Good luck, everyone," Felix says, looking down the table. "And remember, all that matters is that I get an agent after this. So, make me look good."

"Inspiring words, Felix," Holly replies drily.

An important-looking woman wearing a headset announces that filming is about to commence and, after a short countdown, little red lights on the top of the cameras light up and Fred looks straight down into the lens of the centre one and gives a winning smile.

"Welcome to the final of School Challenge!"

The audience erupts, with plenty of encouragement from the TV crew. I feel hot and flustered under the spotlights. Fred launches into an energetic explanation of how the show is going to go, informing everyone that our teams are currently drawing. This round will be the ultimate decider.

"Are you ready, Woodvale?" Fred asks, and they tell him they are. "Ready, Riddle House?"

"Yes, we are!" Felix cries, shaking his fist and getting a laugh.

This is all part of his plan. He explained to us earlier that no one good and boring ever makes it on TV. You have to be a larger-than-life character, and villains stand out from the crowd.

"Let's play . . . School Challenge!" Fred declares and the audience cheers on cue once again, before falling deathly silent as he lifts his glittering question cards.

Fred takes a deep breath. "Round One: Significant Events in History."

I gulp. All that time worrying, all those hours studying. It all comes down to this. I move my hands over my bell. Sandy does the same. She catches my eye from across the stage. This is it.

May the best witch win.

*

They say that it's not the winning that counts, it's the taking part.

And I think that couldn't be more true. It's about team spirit. It's about respect. It's about the journey. It's about the fun and laughter you share with teammates along the way—

"What a load of RUBBISH," Merlin snaps, just as I was really getting into my moving, heartfelt speech. "It's about WINNING. And you LOST."

"It doesn't matter," I insist, attempting to put on some mascara without poking myself in the eye. "I think we did really well!"

"I'm glad you think so," he grumbles, sulking on my bed in the form of a tortoise, barely peeking out from his shell. "Personally, I'm embarrassed on your behalf."

I ignore him and give up on attempting the mascara by myself. With a click of my fingers, I open my eyes to see in the mirror that I am now wearing perfectly-applied make-up and my hair is loosely curled, just as I wanted it.

Riddle House lost to Woodvale by two points. TWO POINTS. It was unbearably close. There wasn't a clear winner for the entire final and our teams were drawing as we reached the final round. The topic was general knowledge. By that point, both our teams were up on our feet with the excitement of it all, hovering over the table bells. And the crowd was going absolutely WILD with every point that was scored. Fred could hardly control the audience and get them to quieten down every time he needed to ask a question, but even he was getting more and more skittish as we drew nearer to the end.

I actually did quite well. I wouldn't say I was as good as everyone else on my team BUT thanks to all the hard work I'd put in the last couple of weeks, I wasn't terrible. The history round, my supposed strength, ended up being fairly even, so no one could blame me for letting the side down. I surprised myself with how much knowledge I've been able to retain.

"If you'd just used a bit of magic for a couple of answers, then we would be celebrating right now," Merlin says, drawing his head back in, his voice echoing around his shell. "Instead, I'm going to have to put up with Casper gloating for the rest of time."

The whole team had been in a state of shock and disappointment when Sandy stole that winning point and Woodvale were declared the winners. We'd been deafened by the support from the audience as everyone cheered for both teams, Woodvale students celebrating their win and Riddle House supporters celebrating our effort. After Fred had finished his end-of-show speech, inviting the TV audience to join him next time on School

Challenge, someone had shouted "CUT!" and the quiz saga I'd suffered this term was officially over.

"Well played," I'd said to Sandy, shaking her hand as we'd politely gone over to congratulate the Woodvale team. "A close call."

"The best team won," she'd declared, before hesitating and adding very quietly, "well played to you, too."

We'd then gone our separate ways, everyone excited to go home and get ready for the dance. While we were at the quiz, the Woodvale auditorium was being set up for the festivities tonight.

I'd been expecting Felix to look crestfallen at our loss. After all, he cared a lot more about it than I did, and I was feeling super disappointed, especially as we'd been so close to winning. But he'd shaken the hands of the Woodvale team very enthusiastically, with a bright smile, telling them how much he'd enjoyed the experience.

"What's going on?" I'd asked him as we trooped off the stage. "I thought you'd be upset."

"There's something you'll never understand, Charmley, and that's show business," he'd told me. "The producer came over to tell me that I had a lot of stage presence and she thinks I should consider getting an agent. We may have lost the quiz, but today, I'm a winner."

He'd then hurried off to his family who were waiting for him and I overheard him telling his mum that they could have tonight off, but tomorrow they needed to start sending his details to agents.

"MORGAN!" Dora had yelled at the top of her lungs as she'd spotted me coming off stage, waving her sign around madly and almost taking out some students. "OVER HERE! WE'RE OVER HERE!"

I'd sidled up to her and been enveloped in a giant hug, her infectious enthusiasm making the disappointment of losing start to fizzle away.

"You were FANTASTIC!" she'd cried.

It had then been Mum's turn to pull me into a hug, repeating Dora's exclamations.

"And you know what I'm *very* impressed by?" Mum had said, grabbing me by the shoulders. "That you and Sandy didn't use any magic! It would have been very easy, too."

"Yeah, well we kind of made a pact," I'd informed her. "Merlin isn't happy about it."

She'd laughed. "When is Merlin happy about anything?"

It was a fair point.

While Merlin continues to grumble about the quiz result hours later, I step into my black dress and do up the fiddly buttons at the top of the back. I smooth down the skirt. It's officially the coolest dress I've ever worn and my necklace, now ebony-black, completes the ensemble. Now that Mum has come round to the idea of mine and Owen's friendship, I don't feel the need to hide the pendant away any more.

As I examine my appearance in the mirror, my eye is drawn to the reflection of a book with a shiny spine sitting at the bottom of the pile on my desk. Maverick's potions book. I instantly feel a stab of hurt.

Maverick *will* be back one day. And when he comes back, I'm going to be ready. I'm going to have mastered my magic like never before. I'll have tried potions, and if there's any chance that I have the crazy ability to create warlock magic, too, then I'm going to blow him away with the amazing spells I can do.

I won't be doing all that for him. I'll be doing it for myself.

AND I'll be doing it for Mum. Because she's proud of me no matter what. She's always there, even when she's angry at me, even when I lie to her and break the rules. She always has been there and she always will be.

That means much more than stepping into an adventure that isn't even real.

"Morgan, are you nearly ready?" Mum calls up the

stairs, snapping me out of my thoughts. "Owen and his dad are here to pick you up. You're going to be late."

There's no denying that her voice is a little strained, but she really is trying her best. I'm still in shock that she's allowing me to go to the dance with Owen, but she told me last night that, for now, he's proved himself to her. I don't know how things are going to be from tomorrow, whether she'll let us continue to be friends, but today that doesn't matter. I'm determined to enjoy this dance.

I click my fingers and a pair of black heeled lace-up boots appear on my feet.

"What do you think, Merlin?" I say, giving him a twirl.

He comes to sit on my shoulder and transforms into an ant, crawling under the lace of the dress and letting out a sigh.

"You look like a witch who just lost a major competition to her greatest enemy," he comments grumpily.

"As long as I look like a witch." I laugh, clicking my fingers and giving myself a matching clutch bag.

Before I reach the door, I stop still, a niggling thought in the back of my head. I turn round to look at the potions book.

"Morgan!" Mum yells up again, clearly uncomfortable.

"Coming!" I shout back.

I make a snap decision. I concentrate, click my fingers again and my clutch bag turns into a bigger bag. I march over to my desk, grab the book and shove it in my new bag, before riffling through to the back of my wardrobe to get Owen's old cauldron from where I'd hidden it beneath a bunch of clothes. I put that in the bag, too.

"You have GOT to be kidding," Merlin grumbles, as I close my bag and rush to the stairs. "You really think *now* is the time?"

I head down the stairs, gripping the bannister and trying not to stumble over my new boot heels. Owen is waiting in the doorway in black trousers, a smart shirt and a blazer. It's strange to see him looking so smart. He grins up at me as I come down the stairs and I get shivers of excitement.

"Nice dress," he says as I reach the bottom step.

"Thanks." I smile.

"All right, I have one main rule for tonight," Mum says, craning her neck to check that Owen's dad can't hear us.

Confirming that he's waiting patiently at the end of the drive, behind the wheel of his car with the doors and windows closed, she continues in her most serious voice. The one that she saves for when she wants to be her MOST intimidating.

"Absolutely *no magic*. No matter how tempting the situation. Got it?"

"Got it," we chorus.

"I want to hear you *promise* me. Owen?" she says, staring him down.

He gulps. "I promise."

"Morgan?"

"I promise."

"Good. I have your word," she says, giving a sigh as her eyes flicker to my necklace. "Go on then."

Before I head out the door, I lunge at her and give her a big hug. She's surprised at first but relaxes, wrapping her arms around me.

"What's this for?" She laughs.

"To say thank you for always being there. And for being the best mum ever." I pull back and look up at her as she brushes my hair off my forehead. "I know I don't make it easy."

"You certainly don't." She smiles down at me. "But I wouldn't have it any other way."

CHAPTER

Twenty·seven

The dance is being held in the Woodvale auditorium, and once Owen's dad has dropped us off, we happily head there, giggling about Mr Blaze's music choices for the journey. We were forced to listen to some old guy I've never heard of strumming on the guitar and singing about Texas the whole time.

That's the great thing about Owen. I was nervous that we'd be all awkward around each other, but we're not at all. We're chatting and laughing like everything's normal. The only difference is we're all dressed up and we're arriving at the dance together.

Just as we get to the doors, where a couple of teachers are standing chatting, we hear Owen's name being called out behind us and turn round to see Felix coming towards us with his date, who looks an awful lot like. . .

"*Sandy?*" My jaw drops open. "You two came to the dance TOGETHER?!"

"Felix asked me before the final," she says, looking very pretty in a dark purple dress and with glitter in her hair. "The quiz wasn't all about competition, Morgan. It was also supposed to be about making new friends."

"Yeah, Charmley," Felix says all snootily, picking a bit of fluff off what looks like a brand new maroon velvet jacket. "Don't be so narrow-minded."

Sandy loops her arm through his and they sweep past us into the dance.

"Felix called me a traitor in front of the whole coach when he thought I liked someone from the Woodvale team," I huff, folding my arms as I watch them go. "And now he shows up to the dance with *her*? She's the worst one! How could he?!"

"I don't know," Owen says, bemused. "They kind of suit each other."

"I thought he liked Iris."

"So did I," Owen acknowledges, following them in. "Maybe he didn't have the guts to ask her. I heard she turned down anyone who asked."

I have to give it to Woodvale – they know how to throw a party. The decorations in the auditorium are completely over the top: a huge balloon archway at the entrance, glowing orange lanterns hanging from the ceiling and glittering fairy lights draped across the walls. The DJ booth and dancefloor, complete with disco ball, is at one end of the room, and tables to sit at are set up at the other end. A long drinks-and-nibbles table manned by a host of bopping teachers runs along one side of the room.

"They've certainly gone all out," Owen notes, shoving his hands in his pockets and gazing up at all the lights.

"I guess they have reason to," I note, nodding to where Sandy is now posing with the School Challenge trophy for the school photographer. "I'm never going to hear the end of this, am I? Even when we're really old, sitting in the woodland examining young witches taking their YWEs, she's going to be talking about how she beat me that time in the School Challenge."

"I think you'll probably both be over it by then."

"I wouldn't count on it," I sigh, watching as Sandy kisses the trophy and then asks the photographer if he got a good shot. "At least she forgives me for turning her into a cactus."

"You know what? Now that I've met her, I'm not sure that was such a bad thing," Owen says, making me laugh. "Come on, let's leave her to it and go get a drink."

We wander over to the drinks table, get two paper cups of a very strange mixed juice concoction the teachers are calling "tropical punch" and go to sit at a table. We then have way too much fun observing everyone around us and guessing whether they'd be a witch or a warlock. It's a great game.

I am convinced that one of the dancing Woodvale students who is flinging her arms around in a circle would be in the witch camp, because anyone with that kind of individual, cool style is obviously not a stupid warlock. Owen yabbers on about how Felix would be a witch in that case, because you can't fault him for individual style. I tell him that Felix would NEVER cut it as a witch, because he's too mean and annoying and all the other witches would turn him into a toad before he could say the word "magic".

At some point we stop chatting and get up and go to the dancefloor. At first I'm nervous because I'm not really sure how you dance with someone, but I needn't have worried. As soon as we get there, Owen starts doing a funny head-and-shoulder bop move to make me laugh, and I see his shoulder bop and raise him a hip wiggle, which makes *him* laugh. Soon, we're trying to outdo one another, going bigger and bigger with our dance moves, and other people from both schools start joining in until even Felix and Sandy are part of the circle, everyone giggling at everyone else.

Mr Hopkins and Miss Gallagher take to the dancefloor too, and, ignoring all the whistles and calling from their students, launch into a very impressive salsa routine. I'm just glad that my spell last term didn't put Mr Hopkins off from his classes. It looks like he has a very good reason to keep at it.

"I need some water," I yell to Owen when I get too hot, and he nods in agreement.

We make our way off the crowded dancefloor to the drinks table and glug down glasses of water before Owen suggests going to get some fresh air. I'm all for it because I'm super sweaty from all that enthusiastic dancing, and Merlin keeps whining in my ear about the "disgraceful lack of taste in the DJ's music selection", so I have a feeling he'd appreciate a moment of quiet, too. I grab my bag that I'd left hanging on the back of a chair, deciding to take the opportunity to show Owen what I've brought along.

We push through the main front doors of the school and a welcome burst of fresh air hits us.

"That was so much fun." I laugh. "Did you see Mr Hopkins?"

"Seriously cool moves," Owen agrees, as we move away from the teachers on the door. "I never thought I'd say that about my headmaster. And definitely no spells helping him along this time?"

I hold up my hands. "Definitely no spells. That was all his own skill."

"What was that about spells?"

We jump about a metre in the air at the sudden interruption behind us. I swivel around to see Iris standing close by. As ever, she looks amazing, dressed in a bright red jumpsuit with a wrap-around tied waist. She's also wearing a triumphant smile.

"Iris, hey," Owen says brightly, ignoring her question. "When did you get here?"

"A moment ago," she replies, brushing him off with a wave of a hand. "What were you saying about spells? I didn't mean to interrupt."

"Spells?" I act confused. "Oh wait, do you mean . . . uh . . . *smells*? Because we were just talking about smells. That must have been what you overheard."

"Right." Owen nods along. "Morgan was saying there are no smells tonight. Which is great. Because nobody wants that."

Iris raises an eyebrow, unconvinced. "Really? Because I could have sworn that you were both discussing magical spells."

"*What?*" I burst out laughing. "Iris, you are so FUNNY!"

"Hilarious!" Owen agrees. "Why would we be talking about spells?"

"Because," she replies without hesitation, "Morgan is a witch."

I inhale sharply. She holds my gaze, unblinking. She's being so calm and serious, it's very unnerving. She's speaking in such a matter-of-fact tone, it's as though she doesn't think any aspect of this conversation is out of the ordinary. That, or she simply doesn't care any more.

This is NOT GOOD. I have to keep up the act. I can't give ANYTHING away.

"Oh wow, thanks, Iris," I say, mock-offended. "Just call me a witch why don't you?"

"You don't need to worry, your secret is safe with me," she says firmly. "I promise I won't tell anyone. Obviously you've trusted Owen with all this, and I want you to know you can trust me, too."

"Iris," I say, glancing at Owen who looks as horrified as I feel. "I don't know what you're talking about."

"I've been having these dreams and I couldn't work out why they were recurring. Then they got clearer and clearer. *I saw you*, didn't I?" she says, her eyes wide with excitement, desperate for me to corroborate her story. "I saw you do some kind of a magical spell. And then you must have done a spell on me to make me forget it or think it was some kind of dream."

"Iris," I say calmly, holding up my hands, "please

listen to what you are saying. You are talking about me being a . . . *witch!* This is completely mad."

"No, it's not," she tells me, taking a step forward. "It's not mad. I've been reading up on it and there is a lot of evidence that magic is real. Maybe you can show me a spell? Even teach me something? I want to learn how to do magic."

"OK, this is NUTS," I say, shaking my head. "Your obsession with all this witch research has confused you."

"I'm not confused at all," she assures me. "Everything makes perfect sense now. The spider that you have with you all the time? That's your familiar, your spirit guide. It wasn't a trick of the light at my New Year's Eve party. I saw you talking to your familiar."

"This sounds ridiculous," Owen chimes in with a nervous laugh. "Iris, we should—"

"What about the bats?" she interrupts, gesturing wildly. "The swarm of bats that followed Felix around. Everyone knows he picks on you, Morgan. And I don't blame you. If I was a witch and he said mean things to me, I'd be tempted to do the same."

"Felix picks on everyone!" I protest.

"In the third round of the quiz, the swarm came along again! Bats never appeared at our school before you arrived. In the two terms you've been here, they've appeared twice. That *cannot* be a coincidence."

"Yes, it can, and it is," I say. "You're talking about me being able to control a swarm of bats. That's impossible!"

"Not for witches," she replies with a shrug.

"You have been reading about this way too much," I point out, praying that Merlin is staying safely hidden. "You've got too invested in those silly stories!"

"They're not silly stories," she says calmly. "I know I'm right."

"There is no such thing as witches!" I cry out, maybe a bit too loudly.

The three of us fall quiet, the sound of the bass booming loudly from the dance. Iris looks as though she's about to argue her point some more when we're interrupted by Lucy calling her over from the entrance.

"Helloooo, Iris!" Lucy shouts again. "What are you doing out here? I've been waiting for you for AGES! Come on!"

"Coming!" Iris calls out over her shoulder, before turning back to face us with a warm smile. "I'm not giving up on this. But I also promise I won't tell anyone. I'll see you both in there."

She spins round and cheerily makes her way to Lucy, who squeals in excitement, grabbing her hand and pulling her through the doors towards the dancefloor. Owen and I stand there in silence.

"I have to say, I didn't see that one coming," Merlin says,

transforming into a black cat to sit at my feet, his glistening yellow eyes watching Iris go. "Looks like she's built up a resistance to the memory-loss potion. The blurred visions have returned to clear memories. Extraordinary."

"Can that even happen?" Owen asks him, aghast.

"Rarely," Merlin says with a sigh, before he looks up at me. "What are you going to do?"

"I have no idea," I say slowly, still letting Iris's words sink in.

Owen clears his throat. "There is *something* we could do."

"What?"

"We could check out some more advanced spells," he says guiltily. "We are a witch and a warlock after all. I know we promised not to. . ."

"That suggestion has my vote," Merlin cuts in, cackling loudly. "Long live mischief!"

"Morgan?" Owen says, watching me carefully and giving me a gentle nudge with his elbow. "What do you think?"

"I think we don't have much choice."

Owen sighs. "We were only given one rule. And we're already planning on breaking it."

"Well, you know what they say. Life is what you make it," I say, a smile spreading across my face as I reach into my bag and pull out the potions book. "Let's make it magic."

✦ Acknowledgements ✦

Huge thanks to the wonderful Lauren, Aimee, Pete, Harriet and the genius team at Scholastic. You have brought Morgan's story to life and I am ever grateful to you for your brilliance and guidance. I'm so lucky to work with you all.

Thank you to the ridiculously talented Jane for such beautiful cover art – your illustrations are more magical than I could have imagined.

Special thanks to my fabulous agent and partner in crime, Lauren G. None of my books would exist without your encouragement. Thank you for everything you do.

To my friends and family, thank you for always cheering me on. You really are the best. Huge thanks to my dog, Bono, for being my constant companion.

Special thanks to my fellow funny authors, the picpoul crew. The most supportive colleagues on the planet.

And to my readers, the biggest thanks of all. I'm so grateful for your incredible support, and I very much hope that Morgan, Merlin and their adventures make you smile.